Gene Wolfe's

First Four Novels

A Chapter Guide

Michael Andre-Driussi

ISBN: 978-1-947614-13-0

CONTENTS

INTRODUCTION

This work is a chapter-by-chapter reading guide to Gene Wolfe's first four novels: *Operation ARES* (1970), *The Fifth Head of Cerberus* (1972), *Peace* (1975), and *The Devil in a Forest* (1976). Each is a standalone novel, and they are different in type: *Operation ARES* being a science fiction adventure in a United States of dystopian decline; *The Fifth Head of Cerberus* forming a New Wave novel of anthropological planetary romance; *Peace* presenting a Midwestern Magical Realism; and *The Devil in a Forest* declaring a young adult medieval adventure.

The Guide is intended to be used by first time readers of each book as well as those who are rereading them. The idea is that we are reading it together, you and I. There are no spoilers, but things will be noted as they are revealed.

How to Use the Guide

A reader could read a chapter of the source text first, then check in this book for the notes.

Or

A reader could read this book directly.

OPERATION ARES

Edition cited: Berkley (pb) S1858, 7-70, 208pp, 75c

Chapter I: "Suppose They Come at Night . . . ?"
In a vaguely post-apocalyptic USA, teacher John Castle visits the farmhouse of siblings Japhet and Anna Tree, and young "Nonny." The four listen to a clandestine broadcast from Mars.

On Castle's way back to White City in the morning, he passes Cemetery Hill, where people guard graves against nocturnal despoilers. Castle is late for breakfast at the city dorm. During the day he teaches his class, and there is talk about the ecological disruption of foreign predators.

The Captain, who lives at the city dorm, gives Castle a hint that the Tree farm will be raided for radio crimes. Castle braves the savage night of roving monsters to warn his friends, but is caught by a "peaceguard" patrol. In a twist he tricks the officer into raiding the Tree farm ahead of time over voting crimes.

Onomastics: "John" comes from Hebrew meaning "God is gracious"; "Castle" is an occupational surname for someone who worked in a castle, e.g., the governor or constable of a castle. Japhet, presumably from "Japheth," is Hebrew for "May he expand," the name of Noah's eldest son. Anna is Hebrew, meaning "favor/grace/beautiful." The surname Tree is of ancient Anglo-Saxon origin, for a family once having lived near a landmark tree or in one of the settlements in Devon of South West England.

War of the Worlds: Not only the seminal novel *The War of the Worlds* (1898) by H. G. Wells, but perhaps even more so the legendary 1938 radio broadcast by Orson Welles, which was localized to the USA and was received by radio. Here the irony is that the Americans are listening to "Radio Free Europe"-style broadcasts from Mars, and they are hoping for a

Martian Invasion.

Chapter II: "A Man of *This* Planet . . ."
Castle's regular class is interrupted by a TV broadcast from President Pro Tem Fitzpatric Boyde, mainly talking against the messages from Mars.

A government Education Team from Arlington comes to White City to give a demonstration. The Captain, having heard of a bomb on the truck, pressures Castle to investigate the vehicle. Castle does so, finding nothing. The next day at the demonstration, the truck explodes.

Onomastics: "Fitzpatric" presumably from "Fitzpatrick," means "follower of Patrick" (not "son of ~" as in the case of such names as FitzMaurice and FitzGerald). "Boyde" from "Boyd" is Gaelic for "yellow, blond, fair."

Chapter III: ". . . As You Must Surely Have Anticipated—"
Castle returns to his jail cell, where he tells other prisoners about the "ghost" that appeared at his outdoor trial about the truck bomb. It was apparently a hologram message from ARES (American Reunification Enactment Society), a Martian colony group.

Later Castle learns his prisoner group will walk to New York City. He is given the option of joining PREST (Penal Reformatory Establishment for Social Tasks) instead of a hard labor group. He does so.

Chapter IV: "I Know Where My Duty Lies"
On the march to New York City, one day Castle's reading class for prisoners is interrupted by a bureaucrat who wants to join ARES. Castle is unable to help him.

A few details become evident: Castle is blond; the nocturnal monsters are wolves, mostly.

Castle meets with Lieutenant Harper who is leading the march. The next day a Martian lander disrupts things for a while.

Chapter V: ". . . Where the Lion Sleeps"
After a six-week march, Castle is now in New York City, where the former UN Building has become the PREST Headquarters Building.

Cut to Anna Tree, who is now a member of a bodyguard team for a politician in an urban environment. She has a compact device with which she can secretly communicate with Martians. On the international front, it seems that China is aiding the Martians to balance aid by the Soviets to the current American government.

Back to Castle on a welfare visit to a young couple, where the man Charley is on drugs again because he lost his job, and the woman Mona is in a primitivist cult called "Hunters." Then Castle meets up with Japhet Tree, who had been searching for him.

Back at PREST HQ, Castle confronts his superior Frank Colby about milking clients. Colby reveals Castle has been ordered back to prison, heading out the next day.

But that night Castle's sleep is interrupted by a suicide prevention emergency. Castle goes, finds his welfare case Charley threatening to jump and take his wife with him. Castle tries to save the man but gets dragged down, almost dying. There is a lion on the street, somehow answering the prayers of the Hunter.

Narnia: The god-like lion echoes Aslan of C. S. Lewis's Narnia series.

Chapter VI: ". . . President Charles H. Huggins!"
A man in space, the Martian hologram model, is in a small orbital station.

Then to Noddy, now a political prisoner at a camp. His nails were pulled off in torture.

Castle in the hospital of the Hunters, his arm in cast, at the temple of the cult. Tia Marie is their leader, and she stages miracles.

President Charles H. Huggins, the constitutional president, is meeting with the Hunters for the first time. At the ceremony the lion appears, then it leaps up and vanishes, then a bull is there. Castle discovers that one of the presidential bodyguards is Anna Trees.

Chapter VII: ". . . Where Only Delight Lives . . ."
Japhet in New York City reads the newspaper about a Martian landing back out near White City, and he moves to seek them.

At White City, the Captain deals with a Russian technician who wants the Rectification camp moved to a location away from the Martian frontlines. Mention is made of General Grant. Noddy is being Rectified. The Captain tries a bit of the process on himself.

In New York City, Castle waits for a Martian ship by the river. Peaceguards arrive and Castle escapes into a building that secretly houses an erotic cabaret. The show of the maiden and the deadly robotic snake goes on while outside noises grow more ominous. When the building collapses, Castle escapes from the wreckages, but giants emerge from the ground.

Americana: General Grant led the Union Army in the Civil War.

George Orwell: The tunneling giants might be rather generic to genre, but something similar is mentioned briefly in Orwell's *Nineteen Eighty-Four* (1949): "[Teams of experts] strive to produce a vehicle that shall bore its way under the soil like a submarine under the water" (Chapter IX).

Chapter VIII: "Power Dwells in the Heart"
Castle with the Martians in Mammoth Cave. Castle takes a test and they make him chief of ARES. The organization, previously a paper tiger, now increasingly real.

The ground burrowing things are "delvers," giant Martian moles.

The plan to rescue President Huggins from the East Coast Rectification Center is an elaborate operation whereby fake protesters (Hunters) arrested by fake peaceguards (ARES men) are to be housed overnight at the center. The job ends on a cliffhanger, where Castle sees multiple Annas.

G. K. Chesterton: This chapter has elements from *The Man Who Was Thursday* (1908).

Chapter IX: ". . . Over Before Sunrise"
Back at Mammoth Cave, President Huggins, Castle, Anna, and others examine propaganda broadcast from the Russians.

General Lee of China arrives.

Castle works on a complex three-way invasion of Arlington, with parts hidden from participants: the Chinese force (subsurface, ground, and air), the Martian force from space (unknown to the Chinese), and the ARES fifth column in Arlington.

After arguing with Castle, Anna Tree breaks away to try and end the war on her own.

The attack on Arlington goes badly.

Americana: Chinese General Lee echoes Confederate General Lee.

Buck Rogers: Castle and Anna in this chapter seem a lot like Buck Rogers and Wilma Deering of the comics and serials, due to such details as the "hovercraft" that flies like an aircar; the Mammoth Cave complex, similar to the Hidden City of the serials; even the Asian ally General Lee being rather like Prince Tallen of Saturn in the serials. Probing beyond the comics and the serials leads to a treasure trove of associations because the original novel, *Armageddon 2419 A.D.* (1928) by Philip Francis Nowlan, depicts an America occupied by a high-tech foreign power, the Han of China. The Americans are organized into "gangs" with "bosses."

Chapter X: ". . . Stand Back and be Statesmen"
The square of Heavenly Peace in China is the location for a celebration parade. A new flag (disc of Mars on Stripes) for the Constitutionalists. The war in America goes on. A treaty is signed.

Now China plans to invade America by the middle of summer but needs Martian spacecraft to transport troops.

Castle stages a fake theft of gold bullion at Belhaven, North Carolina. The plan is betrayed and Castle is tied up. He is taken to the General, who was formerly the Captain.

The next day finds Castle as prisoner sitting on gold crates as the car caravan gets bogged down at a village.

A complicated situation happens.

In the end, Castle wins and sends the gold to the non-Constitutional government he opposes. He meets with President Pro Tem Fitzpatric Boyde and works out an agreement.

APPENDIX FOR OPERATION ARES

Appendix OA1: Notes

Joan Gordon supplies context on the origins of Wolfe's first novel:

> [*Operation ARES*] began in 1965 as an unpublished story consisting of what is now the first chapter. At Damon Knight's suggestion, Wolfe expanded it to novel length in 1966 and 1967. Though Don Benson at Berkley accepted the 100,000 word manuscript, he wanted it cut to 80,000 words. They fell to work, Wolfe cutting the first half of the novel by tightening sentences, Benson cutting the second half by excising entire paragraphs. The result of this expansion and contraction appeared in 1970, its manner no doubt changed by editorial circumstances. Expansion took away whatever enigma the first chapter offered about the chances for revolution or about the true power or even existence of a Martian colony. (*Gene Wolfe,* 17)

Places

The text is vexingly vague as to where anything is located. Research shows that "White City" is probably the one in Kentucky. This matches with the text as to neighbors Frankfort, Bee Spring, Brownsville, and Mammoth Cave. The march to Arlington for the first 225 miles seems to go from White City to Aberdeen (Ohio), to Lynx (Ohio), to Portsmouth (Ohio), to Ironton (Ohio). From Ironton to Arlington is another 400 miles.

Belhaven is in North Carolina.

White City, Kentucky, was a place Abraham Lincoln knew, since his infant brother was buried there. There is a strong Lincoln line in the march from White City to Arlington Cemetery, from the grave of one to the graves of many.

Chess

There is a chess presence to the book, but presumably not as much as in Brunner's *The Squares of the City* (1965), which is based upon a famous chess game. Castle and the Captain play a game of chess (Chapter I: 15–17). Later complicated maneuvering seems chess-like; and at one point when Castle is viewing things remotely, he thinks of real battle as chess (Chapter IX: 159–60). The final gambit with the gold finds Castle facing off again with the General, and it seems, somehow, like checkmate.

Chekhov's Guns

The novel seems like something in the tradition of H. Beam Piper, perhaps a *Junkyard Planet* (1963) set on Earth. On the downside, there are a number of elements that are underutilized, "Chekhov's Guns" that fail to go off.

List of Misplaced Chekhov's Guns

- Wakeys: Mutants who do not sleep at all, represented by Japhet in Chapter I and Chapter VII (106).
- Fistfink: A wrist-locked monitoring device. Chapter V (66).
- Rectification: This process looks like a "Clockwork Orange" treatment to mold perfect citizens in Chapter VII (108); but the experience is ambiguously similar to Martian implant telepathy (113).
- Delvers: Rumor of the diggers being golems Chapter VII (110–11); seeing them as giants Chapter VII (121); reveal them as Martian giant moles Chapter VIII (126).
- Martian Implant Telepathy: Chapter VIII (128–29), "riding" (128), sharing girlfriend's mind (132), sharing mind of dying man Chapter IX (161).

THE FIFTH HEAD OF CERBERUS
THREE NOVELLAS

Edition cited: Scribners (hb) 12830-6, 3-72, 244pp, $5.95

THE FIFTH HEAD OF CERBERUS

When the ivy-tod is heavy with snow,
And the owlet whoops to the wolf below,
That eats the she-wolf's young.

Samuel Taylor Coleridge—"The Rime of the Ancient Mariner"

Epigraph: This passage sketches a horrific nature scene wherein a predator cannibalizes the young of its own kind. It comes from Part VII of the famous poem, set in the scene in which the Hermit talks to others as they approach the seemingly drowned Ancient Mariner. When the Mariner revives in their boat, there are three distinct reactions: the Pilot falls in a fit, the Hermit begins to pray, and the Pilot's boy identifies the Mariner as the devil.

In brief, the entire poem is the weird tale of a sailor who visited the "edge of the world" at Antarctica. He became cursed when he shot an albatross and the ship became lost. The crew died one by one until he was alone. In sight of land the ship sank and the boat with the Hermit, Pilot, and Pilot's boy came out to investigate. Having thus returned from the beyond, the Ancient Mariner wanders the land, telling his history to any and all.

1.01: (3–7) The Narrator writes about his sleeping habits as a boy and how the robot mentor Mr. Million took his brother's panpipes.

Proust: Wolfe's opening lines

> When I was a boy my brother David and I had to go to bed early whether we were sleepy or not. In summer particularly, bedtime often came before sunset; and because our dormitory was in the east wing of the house, with a broad window facing the central courtyard and thus looking west, the hard, pinkish light sometimes streamed in for hours while we lay staring out at my father's crippled monkey perched on a flaking parapet, or telling stories, one bed to another, with soundless gestures.

compare with Proust's opening lines to *Swann's Way* (1922):

> For a long time I used to go to bed early. Sometimes, when I had put out my candle, my eyes would close so quickly that I had not even time to say "I'm going to sleep."

Onomastics: David (3), a heroic name from boyish "David and Goliath" to adult "King David." Biblical David was youngest of eight sons; the Bible does not name his mother.

Onomastics: Port-Mimizon (4), probably from Mimizan, a resort town on the coast of south-western France.

Tree: The iron shutter designed to resemble the boughs of a willow (4).

Wolf, Hidden: Wolf-willow.

Vine: Silver trumpet vine (4).

[Nearly all section breaks in *The Fifth Head of Cerberus* are marked by three asterisks arranged in a triangle; the two exceptions will be flagged.]

1.02: (7–14) The Narrator describes the twice weekly trips to the city library.

French Street Names: Saltimbanque (7) means charlatan; Asticot (7) means maggot.

Shelf Neighbors: Completing this puzzle shows *The Mile-Long Spaceship* (1963), a collection of Kate Wilhelm stories; *Monday or Tuesday* (1921), a collection of Virginia Woolf stories; Bernard Wolfe's *The Great Prince Died* (1959), a novel about the assassination of Trotsky in Mexico; and a misplaced volume of Vernor Vinge stories. Thus, it appears to be a "W" shelf.

Wolf, Hidden: David talks of the fish-trapping weir (11), which is also called a wolf-net or wolf.

Homer: An illustrated *Tales From the Odyssey* (10), with Cyclops and

Odysseus (12). Interesting to note that the hero Odysseus was called Nemo or "Nobody" during this episode.

Abo Notes: David says they would most value "their magic and their religion, the songs they sang" and other details (12).

French: Maison du Chien (14) means dog house.

Myth: The iron statue of a dog with three heads (14) alludes to Cerberus, guardian of the entrance to the underworld in Greek myth.

1.03: (14–18) This was the Narrator's world at age seven (local years). It changed with nightly interrogations, and then he was given a new name, "Number Five."

French: Maitre (14) means "master."

Verne in the Cinema: Maitre's uniform of red dressing gown matches the leisure wear of Captain Nemo in *20,000 Leagues Under the Sea* (1954).

1.04: (18–27) In his twelfth year the Narrator meets "Aunt Jeannine," whom he considers the Black Queen. The night sessions add injections.

French: Nymphe du bois (19) means "wood nymph."

Caught Watching: Caught by a strange woman (20).

Lewis Carroll: Seeing Aunt Jeannine as the Black Queen (20) is definitely a chess reference, but it also seems to echo *Through the Looking-Glass* (1871).

Charles Dickens: The Narrator says that his aunt reminds him of Aunt Betsey Trotwood (22), a major character from the novel *David Copperfield* (1850). This aunt adopts David, rescuing him from Dickensian horror. Naming the novel this way makes the Narrator's brother akin to Copperfield, who is also blond-haired and blue-eyed.

Veil's Hypothesis: When the ships came from Earth "the abos killed everyone and took their places" (23–24). This sounds like the "pod people" from *Invasion of the Body Snatchers* (1956) and the similar androids of Philip K. Dick's *Do Androids Dream of Electric Sheep?* (1968).

Photograph: Showing the couple and the enigmatic house (24).

Ethnotype: Celtic; Wales, Scotland, Ireland (25).

Abo Notes: Narrator imagines abos "dancing with plumes of fresh grass on their heads" (25–26) and nephrite-tipped spears, where nephrite is a type of jade.

1.05: (27–32) The Narrator's childhood ends that winter. He expands his experiments on animals. At the park he first sees the girl with violet eyes. His father tells him he is the heir, not David as he had thought before.

Euripides: "And thence the dog/With fourfold head brought to these realms of light"(29) is David's burlesque on "And thence the dog/With triple-head brought to these realms of light" from the ancient Greek play *Heracles,* at a moment when Heracles is saying that he went to the underworld and returned with Cerberus. However, note that in this play Heracles kills his wife and children in a frenzy.

Four Heads of Cerberus: David's joke about Cerberus having four heads causes the Narrator to reveal he "had always thought" the three heads represented Maitre (his father), Madame (his aunt), and Mr. Million (his robot tutor) (29).

1.06: (32–38) The Narrator's new role as greeter, aided by maid Nerissa. Visit by Earth scientist asking about Dr. Aubrey Veil. Discovery that Aunt Jeannine is also Dr. Veil.

Onomastics: Nerissa (32) is Greek for "sea nymph."

Shakespeare: Nerissa is a character in *The Merchant of Venice* (1605), where she is the heroine's sidekick.

Bible: The figure 666 (33), applied here as a street address, is famously the Number of the Beast (Revelation 13:18). While this adds to the "infernal" aspect, it also carries a pre-Apocalypse charge to it.

French: Adresse d'accommodation (33); Department de la Main (36) means "hand department," probably related to the geographical feature "the hand."

Ambiguous Abo Augury: Marsch's question about aged houses (37).

1.07: (38–42) The girl with violet eyes is Phaedria. The Narrator learns Mr. Million is a scanned person, a simulation of his "great-grandfather."

Onomastics: Phaedria (38) is a character in the ancient play *Aulularia* by Plautus, where she is the marriageable daughter.

Latin: Cave Canem (40) [KAH-way KAH-num] means "Beware of dog."

House Name Variant: "The Cave" is a sight reading in English that is quite different, yet it works well with Cerberus imagery.

Wolf, Hidden: The Narrator mentions "concealing ditches called ha-has" (42), and a ha-ha, being a recessed landscape design element, is also known in French as "saut de loup" (literally "wolf jump").

Dream: Dream of Corinthian pillars (42).

1.08: (42–58) Phaedria organizes a theatrical company that turns criminal by stages. The Narrator comes out of a yacht dream to find himself participating in a big heist job, where the surprise is that the money box is guarded by a four-armed fighting slave.

French: Chasseur (43), a soldier, usually in the light cavalry, equipped and trained for rapid movement.

Samuel Taylor Coleridge: The Narrator's yacht dream seems to pay out on the opening epigraph from "The Rime of the Ancient Mariner" (1798).

Onomastics: Marydol (50) is the name of a village in Poland.

Canonical Hours: "The place was known not to open its doors until after the last Angelus, we had come the next day a little after the second and entered through one of the skylights" (56). This episode is ambiguous about time: since the trio is sneaking in, darkness is assumed; because a cock crows, pre-dawn is implied. These points suggest that "Angelus" in question is in the place of Matins, pre-dawn, one per hour. Yet in the 20th century Angelus was at 6:00, 12:00, and 18:00, so the job is happening after noon.

Floors: Fighting bird floor, fighting dog floor (50), fighting slave floor (51).

French Street Names: Egouts (51) is sewers.

Virgil: Regarding the four-armed slave, David says,

> Arms and the man I sing, who forc'd by fate,
> And haughty Juno's unrelenting hate,
> Expell'd and exil'd, left the Trojan shore. (56)

Which is from Book I of *The Aeneid* by Virgil, as translated by Edward Fairfax Taylor.

Animal Form: The slave as spider (56).

Abo Notes: Agate and jasper as materials for abo tools (58).

1.09: (58–59) The brothers attack the slave.

1.10: (59–60) The brothers kill the slave. David is wounded and they leave without the money. The Narrator realizes he has sleepwalked through an entire winter and spring.

Wolf, Hidden: Recognizing his face in the slave's face (59) reveals the slave is a wolf, in turn making him a wolf-spider.

Mother: "I have tried . . . to find some trace of my mother, the woman in the photograph . . . but that picture was surely taken long before I was born—perhaps even on Earth" (60).

Lovecraftian Sleep Walking: The Narrator's lost time (60) echoes that of the Lovecraft hero possessed by a member of the Great Race of Yith in "The Shadow Out of Time" (1936).

1.11: (61–63) The Narrator sees his face in a slave at the slave market. The Narrator in talking with David, Marydol, Phaedria, Mr. Million, and Aunt Jeannine, and all are talking of killing Maitre.

Rip Van Winkle: Adding to the Lovecraftian angle, the Narrator fears he will awaken the next day as an old beggar (62).

1.12: (63) "Like the sound of a switch, or old glass breaking."

Commentary: "Old glass breaking" here being a reference to the shattering of the mirror as prelude to killing of the four-armed slave.

1.13: (64–69) The Narrator is in conference with his father and the Earthman. The Earthman exposes that the Narrator is a clone of the elder. The father urges the Earthman to talk the Narrator down from his probable murderous rage. The Narrator insults the Earthman to make him leave.

Animal Form: Maitre as red-shouldered hawk (65). This is *Buteo lineatus,* where "buteo" is Latin for "buzzard." The genus is called buzzard in Europe and hawk in North America.

Generations: "You are here [Number 5] . . . I am here [Number 4] . . . the individual behind me [Number 2] . . . was himself originated by the one whose mind is simulated in Mr. Million" (66). So Number 1 created Number 2 and Number 3 (Mr. Million); Number 2 created Number 4; and Number 4 created Number 5. Note that in the creation of Mr. Million, the scanning killed Number 1.

1.14: (69–71) After the murder, the Narrator is in a labor camp in the mountains north of the city.

Ancient Mariner: After killing the "bird," the troubles begin.

Bible: "David had gone to the capital" (70) might fulfill his biblical role as leader.

Timestamp: Mr. Million writes a letter dated three years after trial (70).

Ancient Mariner: "A seabird, I believe a gannet, came fluttering down into our camp . . . we killed and ate it" (70).

Scotland: Young gannets have been hunted and eaten in Scotland since the Iron Age, and the tradition is maintained in Ness.

Weird Terrain: Bottom-less chasm (70); ghosts of friends at the edge of madness (70–71).

1.15: (71–72) The Narrator is released. It had been nine years. Jailed at eighteen, freed at twenty-seven.

1.16: (72) The house is the same. Mr. Million is there. Nerissa rejoins.

1.17: (72–73) The Narrator explains why he is writing this. It is "to himself," i.e., to his future clone(s). It has been three years since his release. The brothel is up and running again. Phaedria is on staff. "Last night" she had "the child" with her, presumably this is Number Six.

APPENDICES FOR THE FIFTH HEAD OF CERBERUS (NOVELLA)

Appendix GWV1: Notes

Despite the "Oedipal" nature, this situation is actually "Saturnal," wherein the elder eats the offspring, just like in the epigram where the wolf eats the wolf pups.

The "fifth head" is not simultaneous but part of a sequence over time.

The "three heads" resolve in the end as Number Five (elder), Phaedria/Nerissa (maid), and Number Six (child). With hindsight the previous set was Number Four, Aunt Jeannine, and Number Five.

While looking over the cycle of generational repetition, it is worth noting the possible differences.

Number One committed suicide by being scanned into Mr. Million. Number Four killed Number Two, which is quasi-Oedipal, quasi-suicidal.

The slave trade came after the war.

Number Four made something like fifty clones, and Number Five is the youngest. He modified the "failures" into various lower classes through surgery and drugs, resulting in the spectacular four-armed slave (crafted from twins) and the mundane sweeper (61).

Because Number Four had time for all these clones, it suggests that as an eighteen-year-old he got away with his murder of Number Two. This is a point of difference: Number Four created clones for nine years; Number Five was at the labor camp for nine years.

Appendix GWV2: Wolf in the OED

Using the brute force method, here are some applications of "wolf" to watch for, from the *Oxford English Dictionary:*

- wolf-spider
- wolf-moth
- wolf tree (this is normally a tree that dominates an area)
- wolf (slang): sexually aggressive male; homosexual predator
- wolf disease: lupus
- wolf: a kind of fishing net
- "a hair of the same wolf" (identical to "hair of the dog that bit you")
- "a wolf in sheep's clothing"
- to throw to the wolves
- wolf-berry: a North American shrub
- wolf-fly
- Wolfland: former name for Ireland
- wolf pen: strong box made of logs, used for trapping wolves
- wolf-stone
- wolf-thistle
- wolf-tick
- wolf-willow
- wolf's-claw: clubmoss

'A STORY' BY JOHN. V. MARSCH

If you want to possess all,
  you must desire nothing.
If you want to become all,
  you must desire to be nothing.
If you want to know all,
  you must desire to know nothing.

For if you desire to possess
anything, you cannot possess
God as your only treasure

St. John of the Cross

Epigraph: St. John of the Cross (1542–1591) was a Christian mystic most famous for his poem "Dark Night of the Soul." This title is widely misunderstood as referring to a personal crisis without God, perhaps being conflated with Dante's beginning to *Inferno* when he found himself "lost in a dark wood." To St. John of the Cross the point was that God is with a person even in the dark night of the soul.

The poem "Dark Night of the Soul" is compact, being only eight stanzas of five lines each, yet it is so rich that St. John of the Cross wrote two book-length commentaries about it, the first one being *Ascent of Mount Carmel.* The epigraph, drawn from famous lines of the self-abnegation that leads to union with God, is from *Ascent of Mount Carmel* (Book I, Chapter 13, Section 8). (Note that Book I, from Chapter 1 to 13, is all about the first half of the first stanza, which amounts to "On a dark night.") Further text of Section 8 talks about "two roads on either side of the path of perfection."

2.01: (77–78) Cedar Branches Waving gives birth to twin boys John Eastwind and John Sandwalker.

Bible: The births of the twins show similarities to Pharez and Zerah, born of Tamar:

> And it came to pass in the time of her travail, that, behold, twins were in her womb. And it came to pass, when she travailed, that the one put out his hand: and the midwife took and bound upon his hand a scarlet thread, saying, This came out first. And it came to pass, as he drew back his hand, that, behold, his brother came out: and she said, How hast thou broken forth? this breach be upon thee: therefore his name was called Pharez ["breach"]. And afterward came out his brother, that had the scarlet thread upon his hand: and his name was called Zerah ["sunrise"]. (Genesis 38: 27–30)

The names match up sunrise for Eastwind and breach for Sandwalker. This makes it seem that "Cedar Branches Waving" might be an approximation of Tamar ("date palm").

Tamar, a widow at the time, was pregnant by way of harlotry, and thus the father did not know he was a father by her. This parallels the lack of fatherhood in the Wolfe story.

2.02: (78–79) The mother of Cedar Branches Waving helps her. When they wash the newborns in the river, the grandmother is drowned and Eastwind taken from her.

Bible: Twins that are separated evokes a more famous set of twins, the feuding Jacob and Esau, born of Rebecca (Genesis 25), but Jacob left on his own rather than being kidnapped.

Myth: Twins separated through kidnapping is a feature of Romulus and Remus, where Remus is taken prisoner by a city, but this capture is not at birth.

2.03: (79–80) At age thirteen Sandwalker takes a solitary trip to visit the priest. On the fifth day he finds the hidden cave.

Sandwalker's Family Group: Cedar Branches Waving (mother), "old Bloodyfinger and Flying Feet" (79). The text is mute on nuclear family terms beyond "mother." The use of "old" suggests grandparent, so perhaps Bloodyfinger is Sandwalker's grandfather and Flying Feet is his father.

Tree: Sycamore (80).

2.04: (80–82) Sandwalker leaves an offering for the priest and retreats to wait for the ghost to visit in his dreams. But his dream shifts to Eastwind on this, their fourteenth birthday, and the twin is chastised for sleeping by his teacher Lastvoice.

Pupil in the Eye: Eastwind, the student, floats on a raft in the center of "the Eye."

2.05: (82–99) Sandwalker hunts and loses his prey to Shadow children. They make him a Shadow friend. He finds an oasis and meets the abandoned Seven Girls Waiting, with her baby Mary Pink Butterflies. She begs him for food. He hunts for her, and they form a family. The ghost comes to him. He sees his family group being threatened by men of the marsh, and Flying Feet is drowned. Taking this for true, he enters the river to race downstream to the marsh.

Animal Form: Shadow children like bats (83), like owls (84).

Timestamp: Autumn sky (86).

Seven: There were seven Shadow children, in the pattern of two, one, two, and two (89).

Onomastics: "Seven Girls Waiting" (91) seems like a situational name, suggesting that "Waiting" was added because she has been abandoned by her previous group.

Bible: The "seven girls" part of the name "Seven Girls Waiting" sounds like the "seven girl" of Bathsheba's name (where "sheba" means "seven" or "oath"). Bathsheba links to King David, which in turn links to brother David in "The Fifth Head of Cerberus." Bathsheba is famed for bathing, and Sandwalker is "unaccustomed" to Seven Girls Waiting having clean hair due to bathing (91).

Adding to the mix, there is also a location "Beer-sheba," meaning "well of the oath," which matches up with this wonderful oasis.

Wolf, Hidden: The honeymoon/honey feast (93–95) seems related to the "bee-wolf" Beowulf.

Sandwalker's Family Group: Flying Feet, old Bloodyfinger, Leaves-you-can-eat, the girl Sweetmouth, and Cedar Branches Waving (97).

2.06: (99–107) Sandwalker travels the river to the marsh. In the night he hears a song of sorrow from the Shadow children. He goes to aid them and finds a few are captives of four marshmen who are using them as bait to lure more Shadow children. He joins a rescue group and fights the marshmen to victory. The Shadow children will eat one of the men. Sandwalker gets directions to where his birth family is held.

Onomastics: Fingers at My Throat (106) is the name applied by the blinded marshman to Sandwalker. This is a situational name.

2.07: (107–108) Sandwalker tracks the three escaped marshmen and then sleeps during the day.

2.08: (108) Lastvoice asks Eastwind for the location of Sandwalker, and he tells.

2.09: (108–13) The marshmen capture Sandwalker at twilight, before the Shadow children come out. After holding him five days, they cast him into the pit called the Other Eye where his family is confined. Sandwalker meets Eastwind.

Nature: The pit (109) seems like a scaled-up sand pit trap of an antlion.

Kipling: The pit from lit is in "The Strange Ride of Morrowbie Jukes" (1885) by Rudyard Kipling, in which the title character, a British Civil Engineer in India, is overcome by sunstroke and goes riding out at night. He falls with his horse down a sand slope into a riverside half-crater, where he discovers a prison village of the living dead, people who unexpectedly recovered after being declared expired. Led by a murderous Brahmin, they live on crows and sleep in burrows in the sand. The place is a perfect prison, as there is no way out from the sand slope or the quicksand and human-sniper of the river side. Jukes joins them and despairs until he is rescued by his servant who has tracked him across the sands.

Myth: The Eye and the Other Eye (112) echo the face of Odin, a Norse god who sacrificed an eye to gain the gift of prophecy.

2.10: (113–23) The Old Wise One of the Shadow children talks. Up at the river two men are sacrificed and two Shadow children are killed for additional food. This because the stars are not kind. New prisoners at the pit are Seven Girls Waiting and her baby Mary Pink Butterflies.

Anachronisms: The Old Wise One speaks in a curious way that seems pointedly 20th century, perhaps the missing part between the 19th century culture of Port-Mimazon and the presumed 21st century level of interstellar travel. "All the great political movements of history were born in prisons" (113) sounds like something from Czarist Russia; Poictesme (116), pronounced "PWA-tem," listed with Atlantis, Mu, Gondwanaland, and The Country of Friends, is a fictional country in the many novels of James Branch Cabell.

Vague Time: The time measurement "Full face of Sisterworld" (118) here seemingly akin to the time between Full Moon phases. The twin worlds are co-orbiting an unspecified point between them, and it might be that they go through a roughly 28-day cycle like that experienced between the Earth and the Moon.

Odysseus: The Shadow children with their herbal chew seem like druggy goblins (118–20), but they also link to the ancient Lotus-eaters of *The Odyssey* (Book IX).

Revision: When Sandwalker says, "I met such a one [drugged Shadow child]. I would have killed him save that I pitied him" (118), he refers back to the belligerent one in the first group he met (84–86) and casts that scene in a new light. Initially it was ambiguous as to who was being declared "sacred" in that scene, and it seemed likely that Sandwalker (as a twin) was the one; but now it is clear that the belligerent Shadow child was deemed sacred because he was intoxicated.

Wolf: Says the Old Wise One to Sandwalker, "You come of a race of shape-changers—like those we called werewolves in our old home" (116).

2.11: (123–26) The Old Wise One talks.

Timestamp: Sisterworld "now much waned" (123).

Jack Vance: When the Old Wise One says, "We had no names before men came out of the sky. We were mostly long, and lived in holes between the roots of trees" (125), there is an echo of a detail from Vance's novel *The Star King* (1964), wherein an alien race of shapeshifters able to mimic humans "evolved from amphibious lizards who lived in wet holes" (*The Star King,* Chapter 10).

2.12: (126–33) The last Shadow child in the group sings down a star. The marshmen flee. Eastwind has Sandwalker help him ritualistically kill Lastvoice, which is required for Lastvoice's failure. Then Sandwalker wants to kill Eastwind but the Shadow child introduces uncertainty so it is not clear which twin is killer and which is victim. Then Sandwalker and Shadow child go to meet the men from the starcrosser.

Onomastics: The Shadow children have situational names based upon their group population in the set of one, three, five, and seven. A group of one is Wolf. A group of three is Firefox, Swan, and Whistler. A group of five includes Hatcher and Hunter. The names for a group of seven is not given.

This sequence is enigmatic. They hint at being roles, especially Hatcher (brood mother) and Hunter (father). They might be roles for groups of "shadowy" teams, from spies to commandoes to hobos. Or a wolf pack.

The sequence does, however, lend itself to hero groupings. The lone wolf is the solo hero, of course, but then there are the Three Musketeers and the Seven Samurai. Perhaps Foxfire, Swan, and Whistler translate to Athos (the leader), Porthos (the vain big guy), and Aramis (the casanova).

Psychology: The Group Norm (128) is another name for the Old Wise One.

Epigraph Point: The ego-dissolving bite of Wolf seems to do this as abruptly as Chekhov's Gun suddenly firing. To be fair, the world-dissolving miracle counts for something, too.

APPENDIX FOR 'A STORY' BY JOHN V. MARSCH

Appendix JVM1: Assessing the Anthropological Fiction

The second section is presented as a novella written by the scientist who was a minor character in the first section. It is assumed to be based upon the scientist's best understanding of a vanished people, with an uncertain balance between "science" and "fiction."

Sandwalker's visit to the priest seems to be a textbook case of a vision quest, which adds to the anthropological tenor. In addition to the vision quest, the text gives alternate paths for "achieving manhood" by way of heroic deeds and sexual initiation in the one tradition, or by fire scarring in the other tradition.

Another strong anthropological strategy is the complete lack of shape-changing in the story. This is surprising, since shape-changing was the main feature of abos in the first section.

The anthropological framework makes the theory of early wave colonists from Earth seems speculative, yet reasonable. The Old Wise One lists four different places: Gondwanaland (the geologist-named supercontinent of 300 million years ago); Mu (a legendary continent of 40,000 BC); Atlantis (the famous fabled island of 9,600 BC); and Poictesme (the frankly fictitious area of southern France around AD 1250). All four may have sent colonists to Sainte Anne, leading to a pattern similar to the five waves of invaders to prehistoric Ireland.

Building upon the notion of uncounted waves from Earth, there is the hint that the more organized group, the marshmen, feeding a greater population, building the observatory, are only the most recent, and that their religion is based upon keeping out new colonists by studying the stars. Unknowingly the starwalkers are working in tandem with the Shadow children. Yet this arrival of outsiders has happened before; and after a while, the new-comers will forget their starfaring ways, and the old ways will return.

There is an anthropological contrast in the way two of the groups value human life. The marshmen kill their slaves when the signs are evil, rather like the sacrifices at Carthage under siege. In contrast the nomadic Free People abandon their weak and dependent (nursing mothers, infants, and the elderly) for ecological reasons. In other words, the marshmen sacrifice outsiders in bad times, while the nomads kill their own all the time.

On the fiction side, “A Story” has a Hemingway feel to it, like a Nick Adams story, specifically “Indian Camp” (1924). This is not surprising, since “Indian Camp” has an anthropological aspect to it.

V.R.T.

> But don't think that I am at all interested in you. You have warmed me, and now I will go out again and listen to the dark voices.
>
> *Karel Čapek*

Epigraph: This quote is the last two lines of a short short story "From the Point of View of a Cat" (1935), originally collected in *Intimate Things* (1935). To summarize, the cat describes its Man, who seems to be a writer. The cat pities the Man who cannot hear the mysterious and magical voices at night.

Comment: This passage, and the story it comes from, illustrate the contrast between rational and supernatural, between human and animal, as well as the imperfect communication between these sides. It might also signal the importance of cats to this story.

3.01: (137–53) An overture. The frame tale is established, an inventory of material is listed, and the first presentation is made of selections from prison tape, field notebook, prison notes, tapping news, and interviews.

Frame Tale: In a tropical location at sunset, a junior officer looks over the contents of a dispatch box.

Inventory:

- A school composition book marked "V.R.T." purchased on Sainte Anne (138).
- A letter from someone in the Civil Service, glanced over in montage.

- A spool of audio tape, among three spools, with three loose labels "Second Interrogation," "Fifth Interrogation," "Seventeenth Interrogation—Third Reel."
- A sturdy field notebook (140–41, 144), with the first three pages cut out by something sharper than a dagger (140).
- Loose sheaf of papers (141), bound with a tin clasp at Port-Mimizon, and bearing the neat writing of a professional clerk.

Prison Tape: Prisoner in Cell 143 (139); Interrogator talks of typhus (139) and photocopy (140).

Field Notebook: The mystery of the cut pages. The pink sun (140), the talking drums (141).

Prison Notes: "Now that I have paper again" (141).

Tapping News: Two Twelve to the mountains (143) is link to Number Five being transferred to a labor camp (69).

Koestler: The prison tapping begins right after the anthropology note on talking drums, but it also echoes Koestler's *Darkness at Noon* (1941), where prisoners tap in code beginning in "First Hearing: Chapter 8."

Frame Tale: Position of Sainte Anne is high overhead (143). Junior officer requests Cassilla, but must wait two or three hours since she is servicing the Major.

Anthropology: The Field Notebook's mention of "Caucasoid Pygmies" in Scandinavia and Eire until the last years of the eighteenth century (144) raises a "Red Flag" of sorts. It describes "Fairy Euhemerism," a school of thought supposing that fairies are based upon memories of a lost race of aboriginal small people. The notebook's line suggests allusion to Sven Nilsson's *The Primitive Inhabitants of Scandinavia* (1868) for Scandinavia and David MacRitchie's *The Testimony of Tradition* (1890) for the British Isles, the latter having a passage in Chapter III about Doctor Johnson and Boswell (1740–1795) encountering possible remnants of this lost race.

Field Notebook Interviews

- March 13, Mary Blount, a woman of 80, an anglophone colonist born on ship on Earth, she played with abos as a child (144–46).
- Mr. D, who says, "Might be fifteen years ago" (147), probably pointing toward Culot.
- Robert Culot (147–49), grandson of a French settler, about 55 (Earth) years old. The Anglo/French war cost Culot's father his legs, but this is prior to Culot's conception. Last sightings of abo about 43 years ago: "sometimes like a man, but sometimes like the post of a fence." (Americana: So, in

other words, it looked like a "wooden Indian"?)

- Dr. Hagsmith, anglophone. He came twenty years before, when the town was built. He tells tale of Cinderwalker, who resurrected animals killed by the new train, and the episode of the cattle-drover's woman (149–51).
- M. d'F, francophone. He mentions a sacred cave far up the river and directs him to Trenchard, a beggar who pretends to be an abo and has a son "of fifteen or so" (151–52).

Onomastics: Trenchard (French) is an occupational name for a butcher or a nickname for a violent person.

Bible: Note on Mary Blount. Her unnamed mother was apparently a soldier/colonist who broke the rules by being already pregnant when she boarded the starcrosser. This seems a dark version of the Immaculate Conception of Mary born of St. Anne. Where the Virgin Mary had a father (St. Joachim), Mary Blount did not have an acknowledged father, thus feeding into the fatherless culture of Sainte Anne.

Frame Tale: Brother officer visits (146).

Animal Form: Officer as owl (147).

Cat: "[T]o the blind, all cats are black" (147).

Cat, or "Frame Tale Poe Intrusion": A cat leaps onto the officer's windowsill. It is a large black tom, with one eye and double claws, "the cemetery cat from Vienne" (151). The officer reaches for his pistol but the cat hisses and leaps away. This seems a link to Poe's story "The Black Cat" (1843), where the one-eyed cat is named "Pluto."

Field Notebook: The list for the expedition (152) is located twenty or thirty pages after the interview with M. d'F.

3.02: (153–54) Field Notebook entry, April 6, first night out.

Constellations: List of abo constellations (154): Thousand Feelers and the Fish, Burning Hair Woman, The Fighting Lizard, and "Shadow Children."

3.03: (155–56) Field Notebook April 7. Frogtown. Lack of tools in supplies.

3.04: (156–57) Field Notebook April 8. "The boy is the worst shot." The boy is physiologically eight or nine (Earth) years younger than Marsch (156).

Ages: If Victor is 18, then Marsch is 26.

Cat: The domestic cat (157). The perspective shift makes it look like a tire-tiger at 250 yards, so when he shoots at it, he misses.

Poe: The perspective shift recalls a similar detail in Poe's story "The Sphinx" (1846).

3.05: (157–60) Field Notebook April 10. Interview with the boy. He has been reading the anthropology texts, but his handwriting, as seen in the old school notebook, is miserable.

Germophobia: Victor's talk on Shadow Children [sic] includes "riding up in the bubbles and the foam from the springs" (159) which gives a wildly different view of Shadow children. Supposedly from an eyewitness, it makes the Shadow children seem more like germs, or the description of germs from a mother to a young child.

Constellations: Confusion over Shadow Child constellation and Shadow children abos (159).

3.06: (160–66) Field and Prison.

Field Notebook April 11: Roused before dawn by mules reacting to mysterious smelly creature (160). Later in the morning Marsch shoots an unlisted animal that is like a water buffalo of Asian Earth (161). After noon he shoots two deer (164).

Shape Changer: The unlisted animal's double pupil might suggest it was a shape-changer that died in-between shapes.

Fire-fox: Victor says the tracks are from "a fire-fox" (160), which Marsch takes to be a fennec (161).

Echo: Garden spot (162) links to location ("the bent rock") in "A Story" (93)

Frame Tale Poe Intrusion: A bird enters the officer's room (164), a thematic echo to Poe's poem "The Raven" (1845).

Prison Notes: The loose pages the officer picks up "these at least decently transcribed in good clerical script" (164), which refers back to either the earlier prison notes he had seen or the Field Notebook April 11. The prisoner writes "I should have an attorney" and describes himself as being "a few years past twenty" (165).

3.07: (166–75) Tapping News and 143's Arrest.

Tapping News: Prisoner Forty-seven tells about new arrival at prison, an old man with long white hair (166). The neighbor "to the left" of 143 taps but does not know the code (167). Prisoner 143, using his knuckles to tap (167), claims to be Political rather than Criminal, which contradicts the officer's statement to brother officer that he is Criminal (146); Forty-seven taps that he is from the Fifth of September political group (168).

Koestler: Forty-seven uses his glasses to tap (168), which is how the main character of *Darkness at Noon* does it.

Prison Notes: 143's Arrest (167, 168–75) was on the same night of his meeting with the brothelkeeper and his son (169), link to "The Fifth Head of Cerberus" (63). The nightmare comedic side of the arrest is reminiscent of Kafka's *The Trial* (1925).

The Trio

- Dark suit, seemingly the "valet of a miser" (169), is a civil engineer (172), assistant to the General Inspector of Sewers and Drains (175).
- Gray uniform, a horseman, is with City Transit Authority (171).
- Green uniform is an army signal man (172).
- "[T]hey might have been brothers" (172), Celestine Etienne their half-sister or cousin (173).

Bad Handwriting: In prison notes, Prisoner 143 admits that others think he has substandard penmanship (168).

Cat: The civil engineer's claim that the next day "I may be an inspector of cats" (172) sounds absurd, but in 1904 the New York health commissioner suggested the appointment of a "cat inspector" to reduce cat noise at night. This is the reading of the trio being "amateurs," but the more chilling interpretation is that they are professional undercover agents who shift through a variety of cover roles, in essence being mundane "shape shifters."

3.08: (176–78) Prison Notes on being moved, and Field Notes.

Prison Notes: After writing about his arrest, Prisoner 143 found in his meal a rib bone, with which he tapped a long conversation with Forty-seven. He also listened to the madman in the cell on his left and almost seemed to hear his own name. Then he was moved from 143 to a cramped new cell below ground.

Frame Tale: The officer is visited by a brother officer (177). The officer expresses doubt about the authorship of the field notebook.

Field Notebook: End of interview with M. d'F, pointing toward beggar (178).

3.09: (178–84) Field Notebook.

Field Notebook: March 21 talk with the beggar Trenchard, who calls himself "Twelvewalker" and claims descent from the last abo shaman (178).

Foxfire, Hidden: "[W]isps of luminous gas" seen in the wetlands (179) are also known as "foxfire." Foxfire related to Shadow child name, and the similar "firefox."

Onomastics: "Twelve" might suggest he is the twelfth generation since the French Landing.

Technological Decline as Progress: On Sainte Anne the old atomic ships have given way to modern sailing vessels (179).

David Copperfield: The hut as overturned boat is a detail from the illustrations to the Dickens novel, in distinction from the text.

First Glimpse of the Subject: Victor R. Trenchard is a dark-haired boy of fifteen or sixteen (180).

Boston Sacred: Trenchard says, "Sacred place like Rome or Boston" (182).

Shark in the Sky: Marsch sees in the air above them a shark-shaped military craft "perhaps a mile and a half long" (186). (For Manhattanites this would be like seeing the Williamsburg Bridge flying around.) This enormous vehicle is a dramatic sign of a higher technology, to which we add the hovercraft exclusive to the military (162), and on the sartorial side, the blue slacks and sport shirt purchased from Culot's (153).

The aircraft initially seems to be the size of a blown leaf, and three minutes later it is overhead. If the size of a leaf is set to .5 degrees, and the vehicle is 1.5 miles long, then the vehicle was 172 miles away. To cover this distance in 3 minutes implies supersonic speed, yet there is no mention of any noise. In short, it moves like a UFO; it looks like something from a Jules Verne novel.

(The possibility remains that this could be a typo: that it was 1.5 miles away rather than 1.5 miles long.)

3.10: (184–209) Field Notes, Prison Tape Interrogations, and Prison Notes.

Field Notebook: March 22, second meeting with beggar and son, with tour of sites the landing beach, the Hourglass sandpit, and the Temple ruins. Trenchard claims his ancestor was called The Eastwind (187). Interview Trenchard and Victor (190–93).

Archeological Caves of Earth: Marsch lists a few (189).

- Windmill Hill Cave (UK site discovered in 1858, having no artwork).
- Les Eyzies (area of SW France rich in prehistoric finds, including Cro-Magnon in 1868).
- Grottos of the Perigord (near Les Eyzies).
- Cave paintings of Altamira (Spain site discovered 1868).
- Lascaux (cave paintings in Perigord, discovered 1940).

Wolf: Trenchard says, "[N]ot in winter when the wolfsnow blows from the mountains" (190). "Wolfsnow" is a curious word, a seeming Anglo-Saxonism from the modern poem "The Loss of the Eurydice" (1918) by Gerard Manley Hopkins.

Frame Tale: Cassilla arrives (193), thus two or three hours have passed.

Prison Tape Interrogations (194–209).

- Timestamp: "[Y]ou [Prisoner 143] came from Sainte Anne only a year or so ago, and you believe war is at the loading point" (195).
- <Tape breaks, so the officer starts another one>
- Timestamp: (first interview by Constant) "From Sainte Anne, a matter of a year and a few months" (197). [This sounds a little before the previous one, so provisionally this is taken to be "Second Interrogation" and the previous is therefore "Fifth Interrogation," making the first one (139) "Seventeenth Interrogation."]
- Timestamp: Came to Sainte Anne five years ago [Sainte Anne years] (198); saw a play about it last summer (201) [fixing it within timeline of "The Fifth Head..." (44–45)]; spent three years in the field (203); spent year at Roncevaux after leaving field (204).
- Ballistics Table: Confrontation about the targeting chart in the book (205–206), but this was a detail already noted in prison notes on his arrest (171), which causes some ambiguity.
- Timestamp: "I will go to the islands next June" (207) puts date of interrogation after June.

Frame Tale: Officer washing off after tryst with Cassilla (207).

Wolf, Hidden: An investigator who sharpens his perceptions through fornication seems like a sly play on the fictional detective "Nero Wolfe" recast as a lecher's lecher, a sexual wolf who is imperial in his hunger and depravity.

Prison Notes: The third time that Prisoner 143 is given paper; in the new cell (ambiguous); noting his own bad handwriting; a memory of school beating by teachers that seems more the life story of Victor with his mother rather than Marsch in New York City (208).

Germophobia: That the mother is "walking upstream for hours to get away from the sewers" (208) before washing the bloody trousers seems strangely germophobic.

3.11: (209–10) Prison Notes. Speculation on location of the new cell underground. Possibly beneath the Ministry of Records.

3.12: (210–12) Prison Notes on dreams, and thoughts on how women are selected by men.

Commentary: The theory calculations apply to running women, i.e., nomads, rather than settlers. Nymphs rather than mothers.

3.13: (212–14) Prison Notes on politics and the dimensions of the new cell.

The Laissez-Faire Party (212–13).

Dimensions: 1.1 meter high (213).

3.14: (214–15) Prison Notes on clues. Sound of bells gives clue about location of the new cell. Clue at Roncevaux that mother had gone to Sainte Croix.

Location: Under cathedral.

Caught: With girl, by mother who then abandoned him (215).

Commentary: Memories of St. Madeleine, which imply Prisoner 143 is Victor.

3.15: (215) Prison Notes on Mother. On how he thought she would go into the hills.

Commentary: While this seems intensely real, conclusively proving the identity of Victor, this is compromised for being an echo of V.R.T. interview in field notebook (190). Which raises an interesting question in itself, if a given detail is echoed in the source text or not, and how that might seem to strengthen or weaken the theory of an identity. Whether it seems to "build upon what is already established" or it merely "parrots."

3.16: (216) Prison Notes of tea and soup.

3.17: (216–17) Prison Notes on bells having rung three times.

Canonical Hours: Prisoner 143 mentions Vespers, Nones, and Angelus (216). Vespers is at 1800. Nones is at 1500. Angelus is at 600, 1200, and 1800, so Angelus is somewhat paradoxed again.

Dream: A dream of his family on a river outing, mother in yellow dress, father with red hair.

3.18: (217–20) Prison Notes on clothing, parasites, and family.

Clothing Notes: Explains why Marsch wore heavy winter clothes his first time at 666 (217).

On Topic of Trousers: Local silk production on Saint Croix, leads to germophobic bits.

Family Notes: Mother knew nothing; stole on her own or when father told her; prostituted herself for food or when forced by father (219).

[The first unusual break "oo---oo"]

3.19: (220–23) Field Notebook April 12.

- A storm.
- Victor, washing in river, had been with a woman (and 20 pounds of smoked meat is missing).
- A ghoul-bear attack on the mules.

3.20: (223) Field Notebook April 15.

- Far into the hills.
- Being followed by tire-tiger and wounded ghoul-bear.
- A mule was killed by ghoul-bear on April 13.

3.21: (223–26) Field Notebook April 16.

- Cat joins expedition.
- Interview of Victor, who imitates Dr. Marsch, then impersonates Dr. Hagsmith telling a story of the abo woman "Three Face."

3.22: (226–27) April 21.

- Marsch is in a tree to shoot at least one of the predators.
- Marsch madness: He thinks Victor is with the abo girl again, that they would "tie," and that he would probably shoot them both if he found them that way. (Note that "tie" is a term for the way that wolves get stuck together when they mate: the male's penis becomes swollen while inside the female's vagina, causing them to "tie" for 15 to 30 minutes. Such things can happen to humans, but it is rare.)

[The second unusual break "oo---oo"]

3.23: (227–28) Prison Notes at underground Cell 143. New neighbor, a middle-aged fat man.

3.24: (228–30) Prison Notes on an interrogation. Apparently this is the same one previously heard on tape (194–97). Prisoner 143 learns that Number Five's father is dead. Thoughts on Aunt Jeanninc, Veil's Hypothesis, and Liev's Postulate.

3.25: (230) Prison Notes at underground cell. New neighbor talking.

3.26: (231) Prison Notes back in the "other" (original) Cell 143. Tapping from Forty-seven gives news; tapping from next door neighbor still incoherent.

3.27: (231) Prison Notes on the best meal and a bath.

3.28: (231–32) Prison Notes on an interrogation by Jabez. This one, mentioning photocopy, was on tape (139–40).

Onomastics: Jabez is Hebrew for "he makes sorrowful."

Bible: Jabez was a man whose prayer to God for blessing was answered (I Chronicles 4: 9–10).

Second Thoughts: Prisoner 143 writes "I let my imagination range pretty freely about my life with my parents on Earth . . . I will destroy the pages at the first opportunity" (232).

3.29: (232–33) Prison Notes on a visit by Celestine Etienne in pink.

Timestamp: Her clothes, "[D]ressed as if to attend an evening mass on a summer Sunday" (232) suggest it is summer. Implies that the whole prison time thus far fits within one hundred days.

Timestamp: Her words state she waited ten days (see 175), then two weeks, then unknown number of two-week periods before this night, a Thursday.

3.30: (233–34) Prison Notes end and Field Notes continue.

Timestamp: Prisoner 143 writes, "[S]eeing my pen leave its weeks'-long spidery trail of black" (233).

Prison Notes: The last page, with declared intention of burning these pages (233).

Field Notebook: Entry about bad penmanship. (Officer compares this writing with that of the V.R.T. school composition book.) Next entry, April 23, describes coming back to camp after shooting tire-tiger, but before shooting ghoul-bear, and how a cat bite to the hand caused bad penmanship.

Cat: In Poe's "The Black Cat," the feline bites the drunken narrator's hand, which causes him to gouge out the cat's eye, beginning the spiral of violence that will eventually lead him to murder his wife.

3.31: (234–35) Field Notebook April 24 a day of rest.

3.32: (235) Field Notebook April 25 Broke camp today.

3.33: (235–37) Field Notebook April 26 The boy is dead.

Confession: Today is not April 26, but June 1. It took me three days to find the cave (236).

Commentary: Note the missing month of May.

3.34: (237) Field Notebook June 3.

3.35: (237–39) Field Notebook June 4 more than a month since he died.

Commentary: "more than a month" further messes with the timeline. How many days to a local month?

Vague Timestamp: Sisterworld phase half.

Echoes: Notes on "the stories" about Free People and Wetlanders

(238) echo elements of "A Story"; looking for eoliths (239) echoes comment from Trenchard earlier in field notebook (182).

Cat: Writer thought he saw his dead cat "flying like a shadow in the dark," which reminds him that the day before he found the cave, the cat brought a little animal offering, saying, "My master, the Marquis of Carabas, sends you greetings" (239), an open allusion to Puss-in-Boots.

Americana: The Puss-in-Boots bit gets even more strange because the offering is a tiny humanoid that looks rather like Mickey Mouse.

3.36: (239) Field Notebook June 6.

3.37: (239–44) Field Notebook June 7, last entry, and the complete cover letter.

Firefox: Robbing snares (239).

Field Notebook: Last entry. Now naked except for shoes, the writer dreamed of Shadow children and a tall woman with long straight hair (240). Commentary: There is a hint of "Snow White and the Seven Dwarfs" to the scene, in a dark way.

Frame Tale: Dawn has come.

Cover Letter: The date of this epistle is nearly a year old; the contents first seen in montage (138).

Prisoner 143 arrived Sainte Croix April 2 last year and was arrested June 5 of current year in connection with the murder of a spy (presumably the brothelkeeper). While the spy's son (presumably Number Five) has been convicted of the murder, Prisoner 143 may still be an agent of the junta on Sainte Anne. The letter offers two options: execution of a spy from Sainte Anne or release of a scholar from Earth.

"We are pursuing the usual policy of alternately lenient and severe treatment to produce a breakdown. Shortly after he was placed in the favorable cell, #47 on the floor above began a communication with him" (242).

Prisoner Forty-seven is cooperating with the authorities, but the material gained "appears unimportant."

The junior officer's reply orders a third option to secure complete cooperation. "Until complete cooperation is achieved we direct you to continue to detain the prisoner" (243).

The officer sends the dispatch box by the first ship leaving, which is the slower ship. The attending slave has known the deadly silk-carding rooms and is glad to avoid going back there by being useful to the officer.

The officer drops a spool of audio tape into the flower beds, among the angels'-trumpets. (For those counting, the three spools became four spools when one tape broke. So there is a twenty-five percent chance that the discarded spool contains unexamined material from an interview.)

APPENDICES FOR V.R.T.

Appendix VRT1: Aid to Field Notebook

(Arranged chronologically)

First three pages cut out (140), presumably covering:

- Splashdown on Sainte Anne (198).
- Military police interrogation (198).
- Staying at the hotel in Roncevaux (198).
- Buying books (152).
- Visiting the university (198).

Observations on Frenchman's Landing (140).
"There was a native race" (144).
March 13 interview with Mrs. Mary Blount (144).
<A few pages later>
March ?? interview with Mr. D (147).

March 19 (? two days before entry for March 21?) interview with M. Culot (147), and same night interview with Dr. Hagsmith (149).

March 20? interview M. d'F, who mentions ruins (151) and a cave (178), as well as the beggar Trenchard.

March 21 meeting with the beggar Trenchard who calls himself "Twelvewalker" and his son (178).

March 22 tour abo sites with Trenchard and son (184), interview R.T. and V.R.T.

<Twenty or thirty pages after interview M. d'F>

April 5? list of equipment, including books "most bought in

Roncevaux" (152).

April 6 first night out (153).

April 7 through "Frogtown" (155).

April 8 the cat appears (156).

April 10 talking to V.R.T. regarding his future; cross the rivers Yellow Snake, Girl Running, and End of Days (157).

April 11 referencing the Field Guide, "single brain shot" of unlisted big animal at a full three hundred yards; reach river Tempus (160).

<The first unusual break "oo---oo">

April 12 boy washing post-coitus; ghoul-bear attack (220).

April 13 a mule was killed by the ghoul-bear (223).

April 15 small child-like tracks around a kill (223).

April 16 talking to V.R.T. regarding an anthropology book he has read, V.R.T.'s ability to mimic Dr. Marsch and Dr. Hagsmith (223).

April 21 shot a prance pony as staking animal for the tire-tiger (226).

<The second unusual break "oo---oo">

April 22 shoot the tire-tiger at dawn (233), bitten by cat during day, shoot the ghoul-bear at night (233).

April 23 write about above, explaining bad penmanship (234).

April 24 eating the prance pony (234).

April 25 break camp (235).

April 26 the boy is dead (235).

April 27 searching for the cave.

April 28 the Puss-in-Boots episode "the day before I found the cave" (239).

April 29 took three days to find the cave (236); killed the cat (235).

June 1 writing the April 26 entry (235).

June 3 higher in the hills (237).

June 4 more than a month since he died (237).

June 6 marched all day (239).

June 7 last entry, the queen of night? (239)

Appendix VRT2: Outside Details

(Supplied by the government)

Prisoner 143 claims to have spent three years in the field (203).

Appearance at Laon—sold equipment (203), including unused pair of boots (207), and sent radiogram regarding boy's death to Frenchman's Landing (203).

Returned by ship to Roncevaux for one year (204) where he:

- Audited grad courses (204).
- Took up smoking, gained weight, found barber (204).
- Gave talks at university (203).
- Prison Notes: Visited a prostitute (211).
- Prison Notes: Found clue about mother having gone to Sainte Croix (215).

Travel from Sainte Anne to Sainte Croix

- April 2—arrived (240).
- <One year>
- June 5—arrested: his version (168), official (240).

Interrogations in Prison (listed 139):

- Second: tape excerpt (197).
- Fifth: (195).
- Seventeenth, Third Reel: tape excerpt (194–209); Prison notes version (240).

The incoherently tapping neighbor of the original Cell 143, said by Forty-seven to be male, is in fact "an illiterate woman who is a habitual petty thief, also appears to attempt to communicate with the prisoner by knocking, but the pattern is unintelligible and he does not reply" (242). Robert Borski thinks this is V.R.T.'s mother, and that seems likely. It is mentioned under the "Three Faces" entry of Borski's "Cave Canem Concordance," where Borski credits Tony Ellis (who mentioned the notion on the Urth List on 27 May 1998).

Appendix VRT3: Aid to Prison Notes

(The "Loose Sheaf" arranged chronologically)

Cell 143

3.01: Now I have paper again; first tapping experience (141).
3.01: Tapping 212 to mountains (143).
3.07: Forty-seven tapping about new arrival, old man with long white hair. One-forty-three using knuckles (166–67).
3.10: Second Interrogation (197); Fifth Interrogation (195).

Underground Cell 143

3.08: Tapping with rib bone, then moved to new cell (176).
3.10: More paper (208).
3.11: Location of new cell (209).
3.13: Dimensions of new cell (212).
3.14: Sound of bells in new cell (214).
3.15: I had thought she would go into the hills (215).
3.16: A meal, tea and soup (216).
3.17: The bells have rung three times (216).
3.18: Silk production (217).
3.23: New neighbor, middle-aged fat man (227).
3.25: New neighbor talking (230).

Cell 143

3.26: Back in original Cell 143 (231).
3.27: Next day, best food and a bath (231).
3.28: Interrogation by Jabez (231), links to 3.01 (139–40).
3.29: Visit by Celestine Etienne (232).

Appendix VRT4: The Government's View

In one interrogation, the questioner calls Prisoner 143 a liar using the quote

A Polish Count, a Knight Grand Cross,
R.X., and Q.E.D.;
Grand Master of the Blood-red Dirk,
And R.O.G.U.E. (195)

This little ditty is from a humorous poem "Twelfth Night (Not Shakespeare's)" in *The Comic Almanack for 1841*. (Note that "R.X." was originally "K.X." probably as a known abbreviation for "cakes," where this poem plays on the cakes associated with Twelfth Night.)

In another interrogation, the questioner Constant asserts that the field notebook is

> "a tissue of fabrications. You speak of a haberdasher named Culot—do you think we do not know that *culotte* is the French for short trousers? It is an obsession of yours that physicians serve merely to keep ugly women alive—you referred to it only a moment ago. And in your notebook you give us a Dr. Hagsmith." (206–207)

While Constant mocks the names as clumsy fictions, he validates the *Hôtel Splendide* at Roncevaux by pulling up a file on it and asking if the prisoner remembers the name of the bellman there (200).

The Discrepancies

- The missing pages of the Field Notes: Something is being hidden. All sorts of information could be here, but overlooked is the most basic data of name and year. The government questions name, doubts year.
- Age: On the expedition, if Victor is 18, Marsch is 26 (156). Yet in prison, five years later, Prisoner 143 claims to be "a few years past twenty" (165), which suggests he is Victor.
- Marksmanship: Marsch made a difficult head shot at 300 yards (161); VRT was a poor marksman (156); Prisoner 143, during interrogation, claims he is not a good shot (206).
- Penmanship: VRT has bad penmanship, as seen on the schoolbook (138); the writer of the field notebook initially has legible writing; after the cat bite, the writer of the field notebook develops bad penmanship (234); Prisoner 143's prison notes have

> penmanship so bad that they must be transcribed (140). The reason the interrogator says that Prisoner 143 would like the notes to be photocopied rather than transcribed is that the interrogator suspects the bad handwriting is an important part of the message, perhaps the most important.

The government thinks the prisoner is not from Earth, that he is a person from Sainte Anne pretending to be an anthropologist from Earth.

The government implies the Field Notebook is a prop. Constant makes the claim that the interviews are fabrications. The missing pages at the beginning are ambiguous.

Maybe the government believes in shape shifters. Maybe in the notebook they see that the Earthman was a good shot, and they see that the shape shifters saw this, too, which is why, I speculate, the shape-shifters directed the boy to take on the role of the man in the hopes that the skill of shooting would transfer.

The government is concerned about marksmanship. The notebook details the impressive shot (161), the field guide table seems to be an aide to that caliber rifle at those long ranges (171; 205–206). The government fears political assassination: in the fifth interrogation, Constant asks Prisoner 143, "Whom had you planned to assassinate here? Not the man you killed—that has the look of spur-of-the-moment necessity. Someone you could not get close to; someone well guarded" (196). The cover letter reveals that Number Four was a government spy (240), and so his murder would naturally raise all sorts of alarm.

If the prisoner is from Earth, perhaps having "gone native," then the government cannot release him. This exercise shows the complex bind that the government is in.

Appendix VRT5: The Quest of a Son

The character of Trenchard's son Victor (180) seems to have a strong desire to find his mother. He states she is not dead (190); he says that as a child he went with her into the hills in summer, where they lived like the Free People, but they never wintered there (191).

Father and son describe her as a fine actress. Trenchard says she could be a girl or an old woman (191–92), but at their marriage at Sainte Madeleine she was "truly beautiful," establishing that she had three modes, at least.

Later, Prisoner 143 writes about her. Rearranging the lines to fit the chronology, when he writes, "I had thought she would go into the hills and so went there myself when the chance came, but she did not" (215), he seems to be stating his reason for going into the mountains and staying there for three years. About his experience after re-entering society, he notes, "there seemed to be some reason to think, at Roncevaux, that she [Victor's mother] had come here [to Sainte Croix]" (215), which suggests his reason for traveling to the other world was that someone had told him, somehow. He reports an epiphany on her leaving in the first place:

> I thought when she left, and for years after, that she had gone because she was shamed by me, having found me with that girl; I know now that she had only been waiting until the milk-task was done. I had wondered why she smiled at me then. (215)

This is the place to mention Victor's "half-abo" (191) status. This is said by Trenchard, who also reminds Victor that he is French (186), but neither means a thing to Victor. A detail in "A Story" that is not guaranteed to be accurate is that the Free People do not believe in fatherhood, and this certainly seems to fit what we see in Victor. The Free People have no term for father, grandfather, or uncle. They have mother, sister, and brother, and they believe pregnancy comes from trees.

Appendix VRT6: A Historical Model

An American saga, the Lewis and Clark expedition was a case of anglophones exploring a formerly francophone territory. The Americans were looking for a fabled "Northwest Passage" by way of rivers. The two captains hired Sacajawea, wife/slave of a French trapper, to help the expedition in dealing with an unknown number of tribes in the mountains.

As the Americans soon discovered, the buffalo lands were dominated by violent slave-making tribes. The mountain tribes migrated down to get buffalo and were preyed upon by the slavers, which is how Sacajawea had been enslaved at age twelve.

Sacajawea seems an important model for the character of Victor in a number of ways. Their ages at the time of the expeditions are close: she was 16 or 17; he is probably 18. Both spent their childhoods in the harsh mountains. In joining their respective expeditions, both were trying to reunite with family members in the high country.

There is an education angle. Sacajawea received a pledge from the captains that her son would receive schooling. Victor talks to Marsch about his own future education.

The Marsch and Victor expedition sets out on April 6. The Lewis and Clark expedition sets out with Sacajawea on April 7, 1805.

Another curious detail is that Sacajawea shared her husband with another slave-wife, whose name was Otter woman. Otter has a link to "A Story," but the detail of a French man with two aboriginal wives is picked up in the story told by Hagsmith (150–51) where the drover sent away the clone who was 100% abo. Does Victor have two mothers?

Here is an onomastic bit: Sacajawea's husband told the captains that her name means "bird woman" (20 May 1805). In "A Story," Sandwalker swims like an otter down to the meadowmeres (99), where he quickly learns to walk silently through the water, "Like a wading bird, he thought . . . I am Sandwalker truly" (102). Which is to say, Sandwalker has a bird name, just as Sacajawea has a bird name.

Appendix VRT7: An Academic Model

The Teachings of Don Juan: A Yaqui Way of Knowledge (1968) was published as a work of anthropology, but critics consider it a work of fiction. Written by Carlos Castaneda, who submitted it for his bachelor's degree in Anthropology at UCLA, the text claims to be based upon the author's experience as a sorcerer's apprentice-in-training between 1960 and 1965. Allusions to tape recordings and field notes play a part in establishing the verisimilitude, but the inclusion of "A Structural Analysis" as the stupefying second half of the book goes far beyond mere garnish.

The method of apprenticeship includes using the drugs peyote, Jimson weed, and psychedelic mushrooms.

In a nutshell, the anthropology student Carlos, on a field trip searching for medicinal plants, meets an old man at a bus station on the Mexican border. This man is the sorcerer Don Juan, and Carlos follows him into the Mexican desert. The text shows the young man crossing over from science to supernatural through a series of powerful drug sessions. One psychedelic detail is of a gigantism where insects become man-sized (this is echoed in Wolfe's text with the Hourglass sand pit being a giant version of an antlion trap, and the enormous sky shark vehicle).

Yet for Carlos there is ultimately a break, and after some years, he resigns his apprenticeship to return to the reality of the USA.

In a 1973 interview with Malcolm Edwards, Wolfe recommends "*The Teachings of Don Juan* and its sequels" (Wright's *Shadows of the New Sun,* p. 17). At that time the sequels were *A Separate Reality* (1971) and *Journey to Ixtlan* (1972).

For *The Fifth Head of Cerberus,* the curious thing is that the "Don Juan" elements have been divided across "A Story" and "V.R.T." The former has the herb that makes Shadow children different (117–19), which seems straight out of the Don Juan herbal medicine kit; but "V.R.T." shows no such drug culture, instead focusing on the grey zone between hope and hoax in an expedition. While there is mind-bending drug use in Cave Canem, it is not voluntary.

Appendix VRT8: A Soviet Model

This imprisonment scenario seems very much like the sort of thing in Soviet Russia, yet the existence of such a sober and coherent tale "A Story" suggests that Prisoner 143 did not die in prison: he was rehabilitated and released as John V. Marsch.

This thought leads to considering "A Story" as being the work of rehabilitation rather than anthropology; about political correctness rather than science. On the surface the writer is gathering all his abo notes for an educational fiction; but perhaps below this level is a coded message about his arrest and time in prison. That is, maybe it is a tale of two worlds: the fairy-like Free People are on Sainte Anne and the trollish marshmen are on Sainte Croix.

A Story	**One World**	**Two Worlds**
The Cave	666/Veil	Brainwash on Sainte Anne
Secret Group	Spies	Spies
The Girlfriend		Mother clone? Prostitute at Roncevaux?
Vision of Mother		Clue Roncevaux
The River		Starcrosser to Sainte Croix
The Trap	The Trio	666/Maitre
The Prison	#143	#143
Family Reunion	Next cell	Next cell
Girlfriend Redux	C. Etienne	C. Etienne
The Miracle		
The Murder		
The Switch		

The notion of an officially approved story being composed by a person still in prison finds solid support in the concluding part of Koestler's *Darkness at Noon,* where the product, called "The Grammatical Fiction," is the sworn-to false confession that the Soviet authorities require. This might also answer to the "complete cooperation" (243) demanded by the officer at the end of the novel, yet that seems odd on the surface. Still, pursuing the thread, it could be that the cannibalism of abos on Sainte Anne is a necessary bit of political fiction for the powers on Sainte Croix.

Robert Borski is on record for thinking "A Story" was written in prison (*The Long and the Short of It,* p. 8).

APPENDICES FOR THE FIFTH HEAD OF CERBERUS (NOVEL)

Appendix 5HC1: Critical Appraisals

Considering *The Fifth Head of Cerberus* as a whole, beginning with selected statements across time.

> Trenchard is quite obviously an old faker, and no aborigine; his son quite possibly is one. Marsch finds hints of the continued existence of the abos on his journey; he also remembers burying Trenchard's son after the boy's death in an accident. Yet he is arrested upon his return by the authorities in connection with the murder of Number Five's father. The authorities begin to have doubts about who Marsch is, and Marsch himself is unsure of his identity. Has the mysterious boy taken his place, so expertly imitating him that he is sure, at times, that he is Marsch? Or has Marsch so fallen under the spell of the culture he seeks that his mind has become unhinged? Is it Marsch who died in the wilderness? One cannot be absolutely sure.
>
> Pamela Sargent, Afterword to *The Fifth Head of Cerberus,* 1976

Sargent sets the table as a binary puzzle.

> The transcriptions and diaries [in "V.R.T."] lead us to believe that Marsch's voice actually contains two consciousnesses—his own and that of the boy, V. R. Trenchard. When the boy dies half-way through his trip with Marsch, it seems that his consciousness joins Marsch's. Or, V.R.T. has changed from his own shape,

> which is now that of someone dead, to Marsch's more viable one. Or Marsch, the dedicated anthropologist, has taken on the consciousness of his subject in a kind of schizophrenia brought on by culture shock, isolation in the wilderness, and imprisonment.
>
> Joan Gordon, *Gene Wolfe,* 1986, p. 26

Gordon expands the puzzle into a trinary, adding a true meld to the mix.

> [Q]uestions of identity are poignantly intensified as it becomes clear . . . that, before the main action of the tale has begun, a shapeshifting alien (the second protagonist) from the oppressed second planet has taken on the identity of a visiting anthropologist. By the end of the novel, both protagonists—one a clone engineered into repeating previous identities, the other an impostor caught in the coffin of his fake self and literally imprisoned as well—have come to represent a singularly rich, singularly bleak vision of the shaping of a conscious life through time.
>
> John Clute, *The Encyclopedia of Science Fiction,* 1993, entry on "Wolfe, Gene"

Clute collapses the multiple into the singular: the boy did it.

> Another suite is made by the three novellas in *The Fifth Head of Cerberus* . . . Because the middle novella is identified as a fiction written by a minor character in the first story, it seems as if we are reading an attempt by a member of a dominant culture to imagine the lost world of a conquered and extirpated culture, an anthropological act that is often accused of being a cultural appropriation. The third story suggests however that instead of cultural appropriation, we are seeing a case of physical appropriation in the other direction, of the anthropologist by a colonized subject who then wrote down a real memoir of his species. But exactly when the second story was written in the time of the frame tales is withheld from us (I think), so a hall of mirrors effect is created that reinforces the feeling that certain questions about identity (like who are we?) are never answered in this story or in life.
>
> Kim Stanley Robinson, "A Story," *New York Review of Science Fiction No. 301,* Sep 2013

Robinson goes along with the singular, yet finds multiplicity when he questions the order of actual writing, noting how this changes things significantly. That is, authorship matters, and even if "the boy did it," was "A Story" written in the field by the man, or in the prison cell by the boy?

•

Speaking for myself, I retain a nagging sense that *The Fifth Head of Cerberus* is "Doctor Frankenstein versus the Shape Shifters."

- "Genetic Wolf" is effectively the "last man" on Sainte Croix, and his clones are the only humans.
- Veil's Theory is correct: The abos took over Sainte Croix (shades of "Mars is Heaven!" by Ray Bradbury), which is why the construction of buildings stopped.
- As a result of these two points: the humans are stuck because of the limitation of cloning; the abos are stuck because of their inability to use tools.
- The fight continues, however, between the human-clones and the abo shape-shifters.

Appendix 5HC2: A Chart

Sainte Croix	**Sainte Anne**
Blue light	Green light
Slavery	Cannibalism
Father	Mother
Cloning birth	Trees conception
Science	Supernatural
Tool using	Shape shifting
brothel	shame

Appendix 5HC2: A Wolf in Sheep's Clothing

My default reaction to the government's viewpoint in "V.R.T." was to consider it merely mundane paranoia, an example of "misreading" the prisoner's various writings into a political framework that was clearly wrong, similar to the political misinterpretations of poetry in Nabokov's *Pale Fire* (1962).

This dismisses the opinion of a very important player, so I work to redress this.

The government fears assassination by long-range sniper. This brings to mind the killing of JFK in 1963, but it was a part of a 1959 best-seller, Richard Condon's *The Manchurian Candidate.* The central gimmick of the novel is that an unwitting American has been brainwashed through drugs and psychological torture into becoming a sleeper agent, a wolf in sheep's clothing, a double-personality with the "sheep's clothing" being his normal self and the "wolf" being a ruthless sniper. To ensure that the "sheep" mask does not slip, the Manchurian candidate cannot self-activate; the assassin can only be called forth by his KGB control agent. In the novel the KGB handler is the man's mother, and seeing the Queen of Diamonds playing card causes the transformation.

With this dual-state agent in mind, reexamine "V.R.T." through the lens of *The Manchurian Candidate.*

The anthropologist and the boy set out on a literally quixotic quest. The man wants to find Elfland; the boy wants to find his mother, whom he believes is an Elf.

Five days out, the man shoots a unique great beast. It may be the King of Elfland. The man's reaction is like the pride of young David holding aloft the head of Goliath.

The more important point is that the man successfully achieved a difficult shot, and afterward a series of bad things happened, just like the events following the Ancient Mariner's shooting of the albatross. The strangeness escalates until the cat-bite incident, and then things plunge into incoherent madness, where the last lines are about a dream meeting with a being one might call "queen of night," or Queen of Diamonds in the Sky.

There follows a gap of three years, and then the enigmatic one appears at civilization. It seems as though this weird one had been away in Elfland, since Thomas Rhymer was also gone for three years after meeting the Queen of Elfland. But Thomas Rhymer did not return saddled with two personalities: the weird one is a hybrid of two-in-one, a changeling of a different sort, a Manchurian candidate from Elfland.

The "abo-in-disguise" side is the camouflage, because abos cannot use rifles effectively. The human side is the assassin.

Following the *Manchurian Candidate* script, the boy's mother is the

Elfland handler. She is sent in advance to the land of the future assassination.

There is even a non-supernatural way to do all of this, in the case that there are no real abos. After all, *The Manchurian Candidate* does it all in a mundane way. I will sketch one possibility suggested by the text.

There was a moment early in the expedition when Marsch wished he could use a military hovercraft to find the sacred cave, but then he notes that any abos along that way would avoid contact (162), presumably due to the noise of a larger group and a vehicle. Yet his mention of "military" reminds us of the strange military vehicle we have seen, the shark-shaped aircraft (186) that apparently moves silently. Such a craft might be capable of a UFO-abduction maneuver, picking up the deranged survivor(s) of a doomed expedition in the back of beyond, and then putting the survivor(s) through the Soviet brainwashing process, including false memories and the conditioning that will cause the personality change to occur.

As for the "Queen of Diamonds" imagery in the novel, I turn your attention back to that rooftop party at 666, where some of the prostitutes wore "gowns whose skirts reflected their wearers' faces and busts . . . so that they appeared . . . like the queens of strange suits in a tarot deck" (19). This happens just before Number Five meets Aunt Jeannine for the first time.

Appendix 5HC3: Calendars, Timelines, Starcrossers, and Clone List

The Year

The twin planets have unequal years, but "They are the same for practical purposes" (198). Sainte Anne has 402 local days to its year (188), while it is suggested that Sainte Croix's "hundred days of summer" (27) points to 400 local days to its year. Both worlds share the same orbit around their star, so they have the same number of hours per year, but because of local differences they divide those hours into different days. The planet with fewer days to the year has slightly longer days than the other.

The Month

On both worlds the year is divided by months with familiar names like March, April, June, and September. If there are only twelve months then each must be extended from around 30 days to around 33. The text is sly for never showing the end of month dates, but this extended month mode would keep the months and seasons aligned. In the text June is an early summer month.

The Week

The days of the week given in the text are Saturday, Sunday, Monday, Tuesday, Wednesday, and Thursday. No Friday is given.

The Day

The text shows two forms of time telling: canonical hours and AM/PM.

The canonical hours mentioned are Angelus, Nones, and Vespers.

"[B]etween the hours of nine and eleven P.M."

Hours per Day

The text is vexing about the detail of the number of hours per local day, which in turn relates to the number of hours per local year.

Perhaps the most solid clue is in the discussion of the boy's age: V.R.T. says he is 16, and Marsch says "You look . . . 17 at least" (224–25).

If 16 Annese years = 17 Earth years, then 1.0625 Earth years = 1 Annese year. This means 9313.8748 hours, and that figure divided by 402 local days = 23.16 hours per local day. Unfortunately, this is too short since we are told repeatedly that the Annese days are longer than Earth days.

If 16 Annese years = 18 Earth years, then 1.125 Earth years = 1 Annese year. This means 10957.5 hours, and that figure divided by 402 local days = 27.26 hours per local day.

(In a previous study, "Naming the Star of Gene Wolfe's *The Fifth Head of Cerberus*" (2001), I calculated the effects of a 30-hour day, which results in 1.37577 Earth years per Annese year.)

Conversion of Ages

	Age	**27.26 hours**	**30 hours**
Number Five begins his new life	7	7.875	9.63
Number Five's injections begin	12	13.5	16.5
Age of Sandwalker and Eastwind	14	15.75	19.26
Age of V.R.T. at "visual 18"	16	18	22
Number Five begins prison	18	20.25	24.76
Number Five released	27	30.375	37
Number Five writes	30	33.75	41.27
Age at "visual 50"	44	50	
Age of Culot at "visual 55"	49	55	
Age of Mary Blount if "visual 80"	71	80	
Age of Mary Blount	80	90	110

Timelines

Four Clonal Generations*

Year	Event
-128	#1 is born.
-78	#2 is born, raised by #3 (suicide of #1 at 48).
-48	#4 is born, #2 is 30.
-30	#4 is 18, kills #2 who is 48.
-18	#5 is born, #4 is 30.
0	#5 is 18, kills #4 who is 48.

* This is largely speculative. All that is certain is that #5 was eighteen and #4 was less than fifty at the murder. Then repeat the pattern for the previous generation. Then let #1's suicide fit the same terminal age, thus setting the pattern.

Three Culot Generations

Year	Event
??	Father Culot lost legs in war.
-54	Grandson Culot born 49 years ago. *
-48	Grandfather Culot saw last abo.
-45	Grandfather Culot died 40 years ago.
-5	JVM arrives Sainte Anne
0	#5 is 18, kills #4 who is 48.

* This is speculative. Grandson Culot appears about 55 Earth years old (147). Using the 1.125 estimate (the 27.26 hour day) translates 55 Earth years into 48.88 Annese years.

The War Timeline

Year	Event
-92	Mary Blount's starcrosser leaves Earth during the war.*
??	Father Culot lost legs in war.
-71	Mary Blount starcrosser arrives at Sainte Anne, war has been over for years.*
-54	Grandson Culot born 49 years ago. **
-5	JVM arrives Sainte Anne.
0	#5 is 18, kills #4 who is 48.

* Assuming "visual age" of 80, then adjusting.

** Adjusting "visual age" of 55.

JVM Timeline

Year	Event
-140	Cave Canem built at Port-Mimizon.
-??	Mary Blount's starcrosser, probably a warship, leaves Earth.
-??	Mary Blount arrives at Sainte Anne; war already over; as a child she plays with abos.
-65	A man from the first French landing dies.
-51	Population of Port-Mimizon greater than now.
-48	Last abo seen.
-25	Frenchman's Landing established; Hagsmith arrives at Sainte Anne.
-21	V.R.T. is born. "sixteen years ago"
-20	"fifteen years ago"
-17	Old-fashioned thermonuclear ships were common on Sainte Anne.
-5	JVM arrives at Sainte Anne.
-2	JVM reappears.
-1	JVM arrives at Sainte Croix
0	#5 is 18, kills #4. JVM arrested.

Arrests and Beyond

Year	Event
0	#5 and JVM are arrested.
1	Officer reads VRT files.
3	Mr. Million writes letter to #5.
9	#5 released from prison.
12	#5 writes "The Fifth Head of Cerberus."

Starcrossers

These starships seem NAFAL ("Nearly As Fast As Light"), putting them in genre company with de Camp's "Viagens Interplanetarias" and Le Guin's "Ekumen." Not much is given about the starcrossers except that they land in the ocean, the first landing being 25 km from shore (187) and later splashdowns at 50 km from shore (198). Presumably they launch from the ocean, too. This is handy, requiring no spaceport or even a runway.

At first glance it seems extravagant to use starships for ferrying people between the twin planets, but upon reflection it shows that the twin planets do not have the infrastructure to make a more specialized vehicle.

Presumably the starcrossers do not use anti-gravity. It is not given whether the starcrossers splashdown in a vertical manner or in a horizontal manner.

Clone List

Number Four made about fifty clones, but Number Five is the youngest. So that means there are relatives, both free and slave, between the ages of 18 and 28 at the time of Number Five's arrest. (The immediately prior wave would be over age 50, perhaps 50 to 60.)

Here are the known clones, in order of appearance:

The mantis, a four-armed slave (59–60).
The sweeper slave (61).
The officer's slave (137).
The arresting trio (172).
Celestine Etienne, a half-sister or cousin to the trio, "a very tall girl of twenty-seven or -eight" (173).

Note this is a list of seven, and one of them is female.

Appendix 5HC4: The Fifth Head—A Novel Solution

In Pamela Sargent's Afterword she begins with the concern that because the book was not published as a novel, "This may have caused some readers to overlook the essential unity of the work." Indeed, at first or third glance, the book seems more a collection of wildly different stories only united by being composed on Sainte Croix: the memoir of a Victorian gene-punk monster-maker; an anthropological romance of noble savages; and the case review of a prisoner in czarist/soviet Russia.

Here I take up Sargent's challenge to consider the book as a novel.

The middle novella, "A Story," strikes me as being a hinge piece as it deals with birth twins rather than the Oedipal conflict seen in the other two. On a first read through, "V.R.T." appears to be the messy appendix to "A Story," a sort of raw truth behind the polished fiction, but deeper examination proves the "hinge" quality in revealing that "A Story" is made up of elements from both other novellas. That is, "A Story" is a hybrid. (For details see Appendix 5HC5: Table of Elements.)

Then there is the internal timeline of the three novellas, where the first one is written eight years after the third one is set, while the middle novella maintains ambiguity as to when it was written. So reading them in the order presented (A, B, C) gives a different impression than if we read them in order of events as C, B, A or even as C, A, B. The ordering a reader chooses is critical for assigning "source" and "echo" among the three novellas.

A third question is the authorship of "V.R.T." by which I mean, not the usual question of who is writing the prison notes and the field notes, but rather who is writing about the officer going over all this material during one dark night of the tropics. The first novella is written by Number Five; the second is attributed to John V. Marsch; but the third is anonymous, either by art or by Gene Wolfe abandoning the device as an affectation.

Now that I have put it so plainly, I hope it is clear that fully two-thirds of the novel is of uncertain authorship.

Say that the third novella is written by someone connected with the case: someone like the officer or the clerk who transcribed the prisoner's scribblings, both of whom have spent time with the texts of field notes, prison notes, and interrogations. Then this novella becomes the basis for "A Story," so we have three authors.

Yet "A Story" is a hinge, seemingly taking bits from "The Fifth Head of Cerberus," so the author of "A Story" must have had both A and C already (thus A, C, B or C, A, B). The material not from A and C forms for B a scaffolding using literary details about Romulus and Remus, Bible twins, et cetera. This is curious, since neither Marsch nor V.R.T. seem conversant in such things. Further complicating matters, there is also a bit of bleed-through of "V.R.T." into "The Fifth Head of Cerberus" (implying C, B, A or B, C, A), the most puzzling case being the echo of prisoner 47 banging on the sewer pipes (166) and Number Five discovering 47 panpipes in his boyhood dorm (6).

These problems resolve if there is a single author with a single goal. I propose that Number Five wrote all three novellas. I speculate that he wrote them upon learning that JVM died in prison, and Number Five felt responsible for JVM having been arrested; a non-target who was accidentally killed in the crossfire of Oedipal conflict. If Number Five wrote "A Story," it is the ghost-written culmination of both the anthropologist's dream and the boy's dream (if either really existed). If Number Five wrote "V.R.T." he had that source material, along with "The Fifth Head of Cerberus," to write "A Story."

So Number Five is like a magpie grafting into his own memoir colorful elements from the lives of others, all crafting a phantom twin-ness. The collection of 47 panpipes is drawn from one detail of prisoner #47 banging messages on the pipes. A more complex example is the dream of a courtyard with the stone column having the word "carapace," which draws from three details: the Dollo's Law (208–209); the prisoner's dream of being executed in a "courtyard surrounded by colonnades" (210); and the prisoner's vision of the burial in the cathedral itself (219–20).

The use of angel's trumpets flowers at the beginning of the novel and the end of the novel strike me as highly indicative of a single, well read, author: Number Five.

Appendix 5HC5: Table of Elements

Tracing elements of "A Story" from sections in "The Fifth Head of Cerberus" and/or "V.R.T."

A Story	FHC and/or VRT
"country of sliding stones" (77).	FHC: In the Tattered Mountains the prisoners made rock slide traps, but "somehow the moment never came, the stones never slid" (69). VRT: Today a small stone came tumbling down the slope ahead of us (239).
The place where men are born (77).	VRT: "[A] stone outcrop . . . which the begger claimed . . . acts committed . . . are invisible to God" (189).
"called him John" (78).	VRT: "[W]hose passport (which may have been tampered with) states his identity as John V. Marsch, Ph.D" (240). Who sought the abos.
"There were tear streaks from the pain" (78).	VRT: Unlisted beast exhibits "a heavy flow of lachrymal fluid that left broad wet streaks in the dust beneath each eye" (161).
"We must wash these in the river" (78).	VRT: In Prison Notes his mother washing blood from his pair of trousers (208).
"[Her] mother was drowned in the shallows" (79).	FHC: David says, "[Abos] drowned the children to honor their rivers" (12). Here applied to Marshmen dealing with captives.

A Story	FHC and/or VRT
leaving rockmice offerings (79).	VRT: "[S]nares have been robbed . . . I know who steals" (236).
"on the fifth day he reached . . . where the priest was" (79).	VRT: "It took me three days to find the cave" (276).
"At his feet a narrow crevice opened" (80).	FHC: The bottomless chasms of the labor camp (70).
the priest's "withered legs" (80).	FHC: Aunt Jeannine's legs like sticks (44).
offering for the priest (80).	VRT: Sacrificing the cat for the dead boy (236).
"His bed was a raft of rushes floating" (80).	VRT: Native silk of Sainte Croix forms great floating mats (217).
"the trees formed only a horizon to it" (80).	VRT: "[C]ertainly from a distance they must have appeared to form a continuous wall" (188).
"the greatest of starwalkers" (81).	VRT: Name similar to Hagsmith's "Cinderwalker" (150); Trenchard's "Twelvewalker" (178).
"long-toothed bitch cat" (82).	VRT: The tire-tiger (223).
"The sides of his head had been seared with brands" (81).	FHC: David says, "[T]hey didn't let their men father children until they had stood enough fire to cripple them for life" (12).
"skin the cold stone color of dust" (83).	VRT: Hagsmith says, "Like people; but the color of stones" (150).
"song the Shadow children sing" (83).	FHC: David says, "[T]he songs they sang . . . were important" (12).
"that milk-gift" (83).	VRT: Compare with prisoner's "milk-task" (215).

A Story	FHC and/or VRT
"Women at the sleeping place . . . said the Shadow children's teeth dripped with poison" (84).	VRT: This sounds like the "mother and germophobia" details of "riding up in the bubbles and foam" (159) and "get away from the sewers" (208).
"you are hungry all the time" (84).	VRT: Blount says the abos were always hungry (146).
"It's all right to play with them" (86).	VRT: Blount played with the abos (146).
Burning Hair Woman, Thousand Feelers and the Fish (86).	VRT: The boy names these constellations (154).
The Song of Many Mouths and All Full (87).	FHC: David says they had songs (12).
Fighting Lizard (88).	VRT: Victor names this constellation (154).
The Daysleep Song (88).	FHC: David says they had songs (12).
"[Shadow children] Dancing around the bones" (89).	VRT: Field Notes, "Some very small tracks might have been those of human children" (223).
counting the seven Shadow children (89).	VRT: Field Notes, last entry seems a similar group (240).
"back of the woman walking before him" (90).	VRT: Prison Notes "there seemed to be some reason to think, at Roncevaux, that she had come here [Sainte Croix]" (215).
"The grey rock gave way to red" (90).	FHC: Number Five's red stone chasm country (70).

A Story	FHC and/or VRT
"an oasis of the high desert" (90).	VRT: M. d'F mentions abo sacred places, "[A]nywhere a tree grew in the mountains was sacred to them, for example; especially if water stood at the roots, as it usually did" (151).
Mary Pink Butterflies (19).	VRT: Mary Blount, who played with abos (146).
"had seen how many children come and how few live" (91).	FHC: David says, "[Abos] drowned the children to honor their rivers" (12), here relating to Free People practicing abandonment of the vulnerable.
(Abandonment) "Pink Butterflies was new" (92).	VRT: "[N]o more than ten together" (238).
"We were all engendered in women by trees" (92).	FHC: David says "They mated with trees" (12).
"At the bent rock" (93).	VRT: The garden spot (162–63).
"He found her . . . among the tangled roots of the tree" (93).	VRT: Field notes on finding body of drowned boy (235).
Seven Girls Waiting says, "No, not on top of me" (95).	VRT: Field notes of Victor and supposed abo-girl, "They would tie, the two of them" (227). FHC: Number Five studies patron and prostitute standing, she watching fireworks (19).
"Drove their young men . . . until fire from the mountains proved their manhood" (97).	FHC: David says, "[T]hey didn't let their men father children until they had stood enough fire to cripple them for life" (12).

A Story	**FHC and/or VRT**
"left their thighs and shoulders puckered with scars" (97).	VRT: "[S]carred terrible" from the Anglo-French War (145). FHC: Scars from clonal manipulations, differing from people "in appearance because of their scars" (52).
"wore grass about their wrists and waxy blossoms at their necks" (97).	FHC: Number Five's abo dream, "[P]lumes of fresh grass on their . . . arms" (25–26).
"The water took him again and he . . . thought of the otter" (99).	VRT: Man writes of boy "he swam better than [any retriever], almost like a seal" (188), where the salt-water seal is replaced with the fresh water otter.
"he caught . . . a dabduck by swimming underwater" (100).	VRT: Field Notes Trenchard says Victor able to catch birds this way (188).
"he climbed into a high fork [of the tree] to sleep" (100).	VRT: Field Notes, into tree at night to shoot (226–27).
"He slept, then woke; and first smelled . . . a ghoul-bear" (100).	VRT: Field Notes, ghoul-bear smelled from tree (227).
"twice as a child he had been hunted by starving men" (103).	VRT: Victor says, "My mother used to say that among the Free People many children died each winter" (191).
"The marshmen were fishers, fighters, finders of small game—but not hunters" (107–108).	VRT: Field Notes, "Surely sometimes, wishing meat, they [the Marshmen] went into the low green hills . . . to hunt; but fighters and snarers of water fowl cannot have hunted well" (238).

A Story	FHC and/or VRT
"They had come . . . big, scarred men with ugly eyes" (108).	FHC: The fighting slaves differing from people "in appearance because of their scars" (52).
"Then men . . . brought a long liana [to lower into the sandpit]" (109).	VRT: The Hourglass tour uses a rope to get out (187).
"We are, perhaps, but one person" (110).	FHC: One in two. VRT: Two in one.
Old Wise One says, "All the great political movements of history were born in prisons" (113).	VRT: Prison Notes "I was thinking of doing a novel, a great many books have been written in prisons" (232). Prisoner 143 claims to be political (167).
"Now humans . . . actually travelled in those, cruising among the stars. . . . We either came recently or a long, long time ago" (115).	VRT: "[T]hey might almost have been the descendants of an earlier wave of colonization" (193).
Old Wise One says "long dreaming days" (115).	VRT: Victor impersonating Dr. Hagsmith says, "[L]ong dreaming days" (225).
"It is possible that our home was named Atlantis . . . or Gondwanaland" (116).	FHC: Number Five says earlier waves might include Etruscans, colonists from Atlantis and Gondwanaland (12).
The herb that makes Shadow children different (117–19).	FHC: The injection-sessions for seven years.
"The marshmen wore necklaces and anklets and bracelets and coronets of bright green grass" (127).	FHC: Number Five's abo dream, "[P]lumes of fresh grass on their . . . arms and ankles" (25–26).

A Story	**FHC and/or VRT**
"My name now [Wolf] is the name for one" (128).	VRT: Victor says, "[A]t the time to fight they fade back into each other and become one lonely" (159.)
"they are green. That is the color of eyes" (130).	FHC: The color of Dr. Marsch's eyes (35).
"Eastwind bit it through" (132).	VRT: Victor says the abos used their teeth to make tools (183).
The natural flail (132).	FHC: David says, "They killed their sacrificial animals with flails of seashells" (12). VRT: Trenchard says, "He had been beaten until dead with scourges of little shells . . . such was their custom, to sometimes so sacrifice men"(187).
Wolf bite (133).	VRT: Cat bite "The cat twisted her head around and sank her teeth into my hand" (234). FHC: Injection-sessions across seven years; the accidental stabbing of David, "[I]t was not until David screamed that I realized I had driven my scalpel into his thigh" (59).
last line "but the long dreaming days were over" (133).	VRT: Victor impersonating Dr. Hagsmith says, "[L]ong dreaming days" (225).

PEACE

Edition cited: Harper & Row (hb) 014699-0, 3-75, 264pp, $8.95

1. Alden Dennis Weer

1.01: (1–2) The writer woke in the night in a bed by a fireplace, but did not know why. In the morning Weer saw the elm tree had fallen, which must have roused him from sleep.

Onomastics: Alden is "old friend" (Old English); Dennis is Dionysius, Greek god of wine; Weer has two options. Old Norse "ver" means "station" or "fishing station." Old English "wer" is a weir (a fence or enclosure set in a waterway for taking fish; or a dam in a stream or river).

Napoleon: A "Dresden figure" of the French Emperor (2), leads to mention of the Ludwig biography (translated 1926).

Hint of Apocalypse: That the porcelain statue is called "Dresden" brings along the shadow of the infamous firebombing of Dresden by Allied forces in 1945.

1.02: (2–8) The season is late winter. Weer seems to have suffered a stroke in the past, affecting his left side. He consults Dr. Van Ness, and is transported to his fifth birthday. Before the portrait of four-year-old uncle Joe, he wrestles with Bobby Black at the top of the stairs.

Mazey Muzak: Glinka's *A Life for the Czar* (1836) is playing in the doctor's office waiting room (3). This is a famous tragic opera in which a patriotic peasant gives his life for his emperor by leading the invading Polish army on a wild goose chase in the woods.

William Morris: Needlepoint designs (6). Poet, textile designer, and author of such novels as *The Well at the World's End* (1896), which certainly fits the mood of this passage.

Andrew Lang: Mention of the fairy tales he collected (6), particularly those of *The Green Fairy Book* (1892).

George MacDonald: Allusion to the stories MacDonald crafted in the style of fairy tales (6).

Dante: *Paradiso* is mentioned by name (7).

Kurt Vonnegut: The earlier Dresden tip, followed by a time-slipping experience, seems like a nod to *Slaughterhouse-Five* (1969), whose Billy Pilgrim, survivor of the Dresden firebombing, finds himself "unstuck in time."

1.03: (8–12) Back at the birthday party, the women are playing at their Indian club. Hannah tells Denny about her own hard childhood, and how she watched his father grow up. Weer notes he currently cooks in the fireplace.

1.04: (12–13) Mr. Weer has a broken discussion with Dr. Van Ness. The Indian Club women plan their artifact reproduction.

1.05: (13–14) Weer puts an elm branch into the fireplace.

1.06: (14–16) Mr. Weer talks to Dr. Van Ness about the stroke he has had in the future, where there is no one left to help him. The doctor says that Weer's future self is around sixty and implies that Weer is currently around forty-five. Weer says the stroke came the morning after Sherry Gold died. The doctor urges him to mild activity, like pulling weeds.

Commentary: Weer seems to be the last man on Earth.

1.07: (16–29) Weer begins the search for his Boy Scout knife. He goes back to the only Christmas at his mother's father's house. There is a Christmas mystery, and for presents he receives the knife and a green book of stories.

The Hunting Rant: One of the colorful bursts (16–17) starts with "simulated staghorn," detours through "races unborn" and fantastic lands, before ending with the "imitation huntsman."

Strange Religions: Within the "races unborn" part is a bit about worshipping sundials and wondering at the term "wabe" (17). This comes from "Jabberwocky" (1871) by Lewis Carroll, suggesting that the "strange oaths" not recorded are a quote from the poem: "'Twas brillig, and the slithy toves Did gyre and gimble in the wabe." Especially humorous is that this phrase was used in the Cassionsville country club locker-room as part of "discussing the round now passed," and yes, it does sound like an after-game comment, completely separate from the context of "Jabberwocky."

Onomastics: "Evadne," the name of Den's maternal grandmother, is

Greek for "pleasing one" and was used for a daughter of Poseidon. Elliot as a surname seems Scottish, derived from Hebrew for "God on high." "Crawford" is a surname among Scottish, English, and Northern Irish for "crow ford." "Mab" is complicated, being joyful and baby and Queen of the Fairies; "Earl" means warrior or nobleman.

1.08: (29–37) Den asks Hannah about seeing the Indians. Instead she tells about how she was awakened by her father pounding pegs into her mother's coffin. Then she tells a story from the Irish girl, Katie, the tale of the banshee. Then she tells about visiting the Indians, which amounts to the last living eyewitness of the last Indian.

Hannah's History: After her mother died, it was the best time in Hannah's life (30). This is the period when her father took her along while dealing with the Indians. It was before he married Maud, before Maud had Mary, before Maud hired Katie.

Banshee Story: This embedded tale (33–36), probably the first one that the hired girl Katie told to Hannah, presents a banshee that is quite different from the usual banshee, in that normally banshees are omens of death rather than dispensers of beatings. On the other hand, the story has a clear and stated moral ("It's not always well to make someone say what they don't want to"), which is a direct response of Hannah to Denny's pestering. But the story has further layering, including audience interaction of the 1800s and "spirit sight" of the hired girl for her ghost-like listeners Denny and the reader.

1.09: (37–38) Weer describes the memory maze of his meandering mansion. The distinction between functional rooms and museum rooms.

Shakespeare: The bit about "nine men's morris" (38) is from *A Midsummer Night's Dream* (1596).

1.10: (38–40) Dr. Van Ness continues. Weer says "This interview between us never took place." The doctor asks Mr. Weer to turn over the first card and tell a story about it.

2. Olivia

2.01: (41–47) Bobby Black dies four years after receiving the spinal injury suffered in his fall down the stairs. Following the funeral, Den goes to live with his aunt Olivia while his parents take a tour of Europe.

Details on Olivia's house and Olivia herself. Note of her three suitors (45), with particulars on Professor Peacock.

Onomastics: Olivia is Latin for "olive tree." Note that an olive branch is a symbol of peace offering, and peace. The surname "Peacock" suggests one who raises peacocks, or one who is like a peacock, a dandy; perhaps there is a hint of color, a blue-green.

Montesquieu: Peacock alludes to *Persian Letters* (1721) without naming it (45). He is romanticizing cave-dwellers.

Animal Form: Peacock as a brown spider (47).

2.02: (47) In the bleak future, Weer tells about the garden behind the room. He quotes a bit of poetry.

Nursery Rhyme Reworked: Weer's "The south wind doth blow/so we shan't have snow/but I think rain is quite likely" is an altered form of the traditional

The north wind doth blow,
And we shall have snow,
And what will poor Robin do then?
Poor thing!
He'll sit in a barn,
And to keep himself warm,
Will hide his head under his wing,
Poor thing!

The full text shows what a sad story this rhyme tells, and how it reflects Weer's solitary situation. On a note of hope, though, the season is changing.

2.03: (47–56) Description of Cassionsville. Mention of island with Crazy Pete living on it in the timeframe of Weer at age 45 visiting Dr. Van Ness (48). The hike to Eagle Rock with Professor Peacock and Aunt Olivia. Den thinks on Paul Bunyan.

General Wallace: Olivia says Blaine favors this author (51), presumably the one who wrote *Ben-Hur: A Tale of the Christ* (1880) while governor of the New Mexico territory at the time of Billy the Kid.

Paul Bunyan: The giant lumberjack (52) was popularized in 1916.

Animal Form: Olivia's hair is as black as a starling's wing (53).

Altamira: Olivia saw this archaeological wonder on her Spain trip (54).

Dostoyevsky: Olivia alludes to the Russian author writing about how murder changes the killer's life "like a religious conversion" (55). This seems to be a reference to *Crime and Punishment* (1866).

2.04: (56–59) Peacock lowers Olivia to the cave.

Anthropology: Hrdlicka (58) was a Czech-American anthropologist. Around 1900 he became the first scientist to develop the theory that Asian tribal people had crossed the Bering Straits to colonize America.

Et in Arcadia ego: The human skull in the cave (58) hints at the painting *Et in Arcadia ego* (1637) by Poussin.

2.05: (59–68) Olivia's second suitor is James Macafee, owner of the department store. Mention of the Chinese Egg affair. The story of princess Elaia. Den as Olivia's dog tender, i.e., dog boy.

Onomastics: Macafee (59), presumably from McAfee, is Irish/Scottish, meaning "son of black peace."

Princess Elaia: This embedded story (61–64) seems the type of fairy tale to be found in a collection by Andrew Lang, yet it is not. The tale appears to be about Aunt Olivia, and "Elaia" is Greek for "olive branch." Just as Olivia has three suitors, so does the princess, each linked to a different element (earth, water, and air), but the mysterious visitor in wolfskin says that fire will win Elaia. The tale breaks off just after the princess has rejected the three suitors, at a moment when Aunt Olivia calls to Den to go to sleep.

Timestamp: Height of the warlord period, when the death of Yuan Shikai (1859–1916) left China leaderless (66), means the date is sometime after 1916.

Gilbert and Sullivan: Den's line "If you want to know who we are/We are gentlemen of Japan" is from *The Mikado* (1885).

The Fornicating Rant: Another hallucinatory vision (67–68), beginning with general "male-female coupling" before getting detailed and specific with teenagers Melissa and Ted, and Ted and Lisa.

2.06: (68–72) Weer writes "I wrote last night." His dream of the garden and being twenty-five. Back to his telling of Olivia and Macafee, when Den was "eight or early nine," and the season turned to summer.

2.07: (72–80) First word of the Chinese Egg comes from Mrs. Brice. Stewart Blaine had seen the egg, and describes it. In order to get more information on the Egg, Eleanor Bold goes to a church picnic with Dick Porter, much to his astonishment, and there she finds the Egg's owner and prepares the way for its sale. At Judge Bold's house, Macafee tells Eleanor his intention to buy it for Olivia's birthday. Sensing a plot, Olivia tells Eleanor her plan to get cash for the egg from Blaine.

Onomastics: Brice (73) is Celtic for "swift."

Charles Dickens: Mentioned as discussed by Macafee and Judge Bold (79).

Anthony Trollope: Named as Judge Bold's favorite author (79). This is curious, since one of his two daughters is named Eleanor, and Eleanor Bold is a character in Trollope's novel *Barchester Towers* (1857), where she is a wealthy widow who has three potential suitors: Obadiah Slope (a sycophant; a lineal descendant of Doctor Slop from *Tristam Shandy* (1767)), Bertie Stanhope (an artist), and Francis Arabin (a vicar, formerly a professor). This literary detail gives a possible clue to the pattern of Olivia's three suitors.

Animal Forms: Eleanor as a minx (78), Eleanor as a goose (80).

2.08: (80–3) Visiting Stewart Blaine's house. Bank-owning Blaine is the third of Olivia's three suitors.

Onomastics: Blaine (81) is Scottish-Gaelic for "yellow."

Automobiles: Peacock's car is hidden; Blaine's is a British luxury car.

2.09: (83–91) "Between this paragraph and the last . . ." Weer's discoveries in the memory mansion include the Persian room, which was never in the plans.

Back at Blaine's house, Doherty tells Denny about old Kate. After dinner, Doherty recounts for Denny a tale from old Kate, a story about Finn M'Cool and St. Brandon's boat.

Onomastics: Doherty (85) is Irish for "Destroyer in Battle."

Ralph Waldo Emerson: Blaine realized he knew more about Emerson than his professor did (87). Since Emerson was a founder of Transcendentalism, this provides a key to Blaine's ethereal nature.

Alma Mater: Olivia's college was not Radcliffe but Adelphi (87), which was located in Brooklyn and was a women's college after 1912.

St. Brandon: Doherty's story (88–91) is ostensibly a parody of *Navigation of St. Brendan* (circa 950), a romance based upon legendary voyages sometime in 512–530, but Doherty includes other surprises as well.

- Finn M'Cool: Finn (88) is the hero of the Fenian Cycle of Celtic myth.
- Hollywood: Strongheart (88) is the name of the first major canine film star. He appeared in outdoor adventure films, including *The Silent Call* (1921) and *White Fang* (1925).
- St. Brandon: Also known as "Brendan," and "the Navigator," this saint was searching for the Isle of the Blessed, and there is speculation that he discovered America.

- Irish Bull: The idea of a boat being made of stone (88) seems like a tall tale absurdity.
- Geology and Geography: The description of a "stone boat" stretching from Bantry Bay of Ireland to Boston Bay of America would more accurately apply to a land bridge, like the legendary Giant's Causeway connecting Ireland to Scotland (a bridge built by Finn M'Cool in one story) or the Beringia land bridge connecting Asia to Alaska during the ice age (a theory pioneered by Hrdlicka, mentioned here before). That the story uses the timespan "twenty thousand years" (90) would fit this time frame; "[t]hen the boat sank" (91) as the rising water covered the bridge by 9000 BC.
- Kilkenny Cats: The fight between cat and rat comes from the Irish bull "Kilkenny Cats" (1807), but here the combat between wickedness and fairy has their pieces running off into the woods.

2.10: (91–93) The car trip to the Lorn farm. Den in the rumble seat sees a pillar cloud ahead. The whiteness makes him think on the mast of Brandon's ship, and then of Princess Elaia's tower, but then it abruptly turns black, which starts off the next embedded story.

Automobiles: Macafee's car is a coupe with a rumble seat.

2.11: (93–96) The tale of ben Yahya and the marid. The hero, through an accident, is bound to work tirelessly for his master for thirty years in exchange for the woman he loved at first sight. The hero gets through this labor sentence and is magically transported to the Haunted City, where the story breaks off since dawn has come to Shahrazad's frame tale.

Commentary: This story seems like an Arabian Nights tale collected by Andrew Lang, but it is not.

Onomastics: The hero's name "ben Yahya" means "son of John," and the marid's name "Naranj" means "orange."

Bible: The motif of a man working years to earn a promised bride can be found in the Old Testament's account of Jacob and Rachel (Genesis 29:18–28). In that text, Jacob serves seven years for Rachel, but her father substitutes her older sister Leah; Jacob then serves another seven years for Rachel. (Note that Jacob, through his wives, becomes the father of the twelve tribes of Israel.)

2.12: (96–113) Arrival at the Lorn farm in the pouring rain. The hunt for the Chinese Egg. The finding of the Chinese Egg by Den and Margaret Lorn.

3. The Alchemist

3.01: (114–16) Weer's musing on his high school romance with Margaret Lorn is interrupted by Dr. Van Ness and his TAT cards. Something has changed, since now the doctor refers to Weer as being the president of his company. The doctor shows him a card, asks for a description ("There's a woman—at least I think it's a woman, it might be a boy, an adolescent. She's handing that other one something."), and then asks for a story.

Psychology: The Thematic Apperception Test, developed in the 1930s, uses TAT cards (115), a set of 31 cards showing provocative yet ambiguous images. However, through research I am unable to find a TAT card with the described image.

Tarot: When Weer says, "The fool. One of the greater trumps—some say second only to the juggler" (115) he reveals a surprising knowledge of Tarot, where The Fool is card zero and The Juggler is card one. It is unclear where Weer picked up this occult knowledge, but Gene Wolfe wrote on the topic an award-winning poem, "The Computer Iterates the Greater Trumps" (1978). The greater trumps is a set of 22 cards. Weer is making the assumption that TAT cards are related to Tarot cards, which is a provocative idea. Even so, there is no Tarot card with the described image.

3.02: (116–17) The tale of the china pillow. The young hero sets out. The old man shows him the ceramic pillow.

3.03: (117–18) Blaine interrupts the story. Conversation reveals that Olivia is telling the story. Peacock's friend Julius Smart is also there.

Onomastics: The surname "Smart" (118) maintains its modern senses across many centuries, being in Middle English "smart" for "quick, prompt"; and in Old English "smeart" for "stinging, painful," from "smeortan," meaning "to sting."

3.04: (118) The china pillow, part two. The young hero sleeps with his head on the pillow, but in the morning the pillow and the old man are gone.

3.05: (118) Den asks a question.

3.06: (118) The china pillow, part three. The young hero gets to the city.

3.07: (119) Birthday boy Macafee jokes.

3.08: (119–20) The china pillow, part four. The young hero has a glorious career.

3.09: (120) Eleanor Bold comments.

Commentary: There are seven people at the party.

3.10: (120–21) The china pillow, part five. The mature hero gets lost chasing a wolf. He finds a small cave with an old man who allows him to stay. The hero admits he wishes he could relive his first day of adventure again. He wakes up and it is so.

Olivia's Subtext: Her message to James Macafee is that he could have won Olivia, but he chose the porcelain egg instead.

Chinese Literature: Olivia's story shows a certain resemblance to "The Dream of the Yellow Millet," a legend about Lu Dongbin, alchemist of the Tang dynasty. In this dream he lived a future life, first rising to prestige, then falling to his dying on the street as a pauper, at which moment he awoke to find that he had experienced the entire eighteen years in the mere minutes it took his millet to cook. (However, this legend has no magical headrest.)

Bible: A supernatural pillow appears in the Old Testament when Jacob, at the beginning of his life away from home, left Beer-sheba and went toward Haran. When night fell, he took a stone for a pillow, and then he dreamed of a ladder reaching up to heaven, and saw the angels of God coming and going upon it. Then God was beside him, and promised him the land he was on, for himself and his descendants. When Jacob woke up, he named the place Bethel, meaning "House of God" (Genesis 28:10–19).

3.11: (121) Interlude of spin the bottle to select the next story-teller.

Commentary: Note that "spin the bottle" is normally used for a kissing game. In its own way, this storytelling game turns out to be a courtship tournament of a similar type.

3.12: (121–23) Context of Julius Smart, who married Olivia. He first bought the old drug store, beginning a transformation of the whole town.

3.13: (123–24) Smart's tale of Tilly. A true story that happened to him the year he graduated with a pharmacy degree.

3.14: (124) Olivia's interruption.

3.15: (124–26) The tale of Tilly, part two. He searched far and wide before finding a place in Florida. During his interview with Mr. Tilly, a woman with no arms entered the store.

Shakespeare: Tilly had a high forehead like Shakespeare.

3.16: (126) Eleanor's interruption.

3.17: (126–27) The tale of Tilly, part three. The armless woman bought a parcel and left.

3.18: (127) Peacock's interruption.

3.19: (127) The tale of Tilly, part four. A man in a car drove the armless woman away.

3.20: (127) Olivia's second interruption.

3.21: (127–29) The tale of Tilly, part five. Tilly took Smart to breakfast, but switched their meals at the last minute.

3.22: (129–30) Audience discusses puzzle.

3.23: (130–32) The tale of Tilly, part six. Tilly had Smart mind the store, then go to Tilly's house with groceries. Smart felt watched from the house.

3.24: (132–33) Blaine's interruption.

3.25: (133–37) The tale of Tilly, part seven. Smart made dinner. Tilly showed his concern about being poisoned. At night Smart awoke feeling watched.

3.26: (137) Eleanor's interruption.

3.27: (137–39) The tale of Tilly, part eight. He encountered Tilly, who had also heard something. Tilly showed him the petrified flesh of his side.

Bible: Touching Tilly's side (139) is similar to the action of touching the wound in the side of Jesus.

3.28: (139) Olivia's third interruption.

3.29: (139–41) The tale of Tilly, part nine. Tilly admitted he was a haunted man.

3.30: (141–42) Audience interruption.

3.31: (142–44) The tale of Tilly, part ten. The next day, Smart saw further signs of Tilly's petrification.

3.32: (144) Olivia's fourth interruption, where she gives answer to puzzle.

3.33: (144–45) Weer digresses on his attempt at telling this story to Bill Batton thirty-five or forty years later (i.e., at the age of 44 to 49). Inspired by this memory, Weer sets forth to find the office replica.

3.34: (145–46) Weer finds the historical room based on his presidential office. Talk with Bill Batton leads to memory of the Olivia and Julius Smart wedding. This provokes Weer to conclude the Chinese Egg Hunt story with Olivia's pyrrhic victory of buying the Egg at the Lorn farm.

Commentary: Olivia bought the Egg but had to give it as birthday present to Macafee, so she had won the battle but lost the war. Still, it is this action that matches the TAT Card ("There's a woman—at least I think it's a woman, it might be a boy, an adolescent. She's handing that other one something.") that set off the tale (116).

3:35: (147) Olivia demands the tale of Tilly continue.

Commentary: Layering worthy of Shahrazad. Bravo!

3:36: (147) The tale of Tilly, part eleven. Smart was working the store alone when a startling customer arrived.

3.37: (147) Eleanor Bold answers question.

3.38: (147–54) The tale of Tilly, part twelve. The return of the armless woman. By force she took Smart to see her son Charlie for some medical emergency. Smart learned that Tilly was a freak-maker, and Charlie was taking "medicine" to make him into a dog boy.

3.39: (154) Olivia's fifth interruption.

3.40: (154–55) The tale of Tilly, part thirteen. The freak Litho told Smart he takes a medicine to create his stone flesh, but he watches his dosage.

3.41: (155–57) Olivia's sixth interruption, where she calls Den to go to bed. Weer digresses, recounting the time in high school he told the tale of Tilly to Margaret Lorn on their picnic by the river. Then the dream he had that night, where he told Margaret that his father would take the dog boy hunting. Den pleads that the story continue.

The Walking Stonemen Rant: Den finds new horror in the familiar tale of Tilly.

3.42: (157) The tale of Tilly, part fourteen. Smart confronts Tilly. Tilly said he had destroyed the stone-flesh stuff, but the ghost must still have a bottle of it.

3.43: (159–60) Den interrupts, and the tale continues to the death of Tilly. Weer offers digression on Smart's physical appearance at three distinct stages: the elderly founder of a corporation; the much younger man at Olivia's funeral; and the twenty-year-old at Macafee's party, telling the story.

3.44: (160–61) Back to the tale of Tilly, about finding Tilly dead. It was on the sixth morning. No answer to knocks.

3.45: (161) Den interrupts.

3.46: (161) The tale of Tilly, part seventeen. Smart entered through window, examined corpse, called doctor.

3.47: (161) Eleanor interrupts.

3.48: (162) The tale of Tilly, part eighteen. Smart stayed on to run the store until Tilly's relatives sold it.

3.49: (162) Olivia's seventh interruption.

3.50: (162) Smart responds. He used the money he earned there to buy the store in Cassionsville.

3.51: (162) Olivia replies.

3.52: (162) The tale of Tilly, part nineteen. They sold Tilly's store and Smart moved away.

3.53: (162) Weer interrupts to report having heard a door close in the sprawling mansion museum.

3.54: (163–65) Denny, four years old, at Dr. Black's office.

Timestamp: At the doctor's office Denny's mother is reading *Liberty* magazine, a Seventh Day Adventist publication beginning in 1906. This is a paradox to the timeline if it is instead the general audience magazine of the same name that ran from 1924 to 1950.

4. Gold

4.01: (166) Dr. Van Ness shows Weer a second TAT card ("[A] figure writes at a table, another peers over his shoulder") and inspires a new story.

Psychology: As before, I am unable to find a TAT card with the described image. Nor is there a Tarot card matching this.

4.02: (166–73) About the family Gold. Aaron Gold asks adult Weer about pricing for a rare book. Weer visits the public library to research Amanda Ros. The library was formerly Olivia's house.

Amanda Ros: An Irish writer (1860–1939), famous for being exceptionally bad. Author of novels *Irene Iddesleigh* (1897), *Delina Delaney* (1898), and *Donald Dudley, the Bastard Critic* (1900); poet of collections *Poems of Puncture* (1912) and *Fumes of Formation* (1933). Then there is "*Helen Huddleston* (unfinished at the time of her death in 1936 [sic]; as was the similarly promising *The Lusty Lawyer*)" (Sutherland, *Curiosities of Literature*, 2009, p. 93).

Timestamp: Twenty-five years after Olivia's death (169); Jack Loudan's biography *O Rare Amanda!* (1954) gives a date of being after 1954.

4.03: (173) Weer's introspection.

4.04: (173–74) Back at the library, asking the librarian to dinner.

4.05: (174) What was her name?

4.06: (174–80) That evening when she gets off work. They talk about the Kate Boyne diary.

Timestamp: Buckskin forgery forty years ago (175); knife was Christmas at six (176). So Weer at library is 45 years old.

James Branch Cabell: Librarian Lois makes reference (176) to Cabell's infamous *Jurgen, A Comedy of Justice* (1919). This is bookish flirtation, since *Jurgen* is known for double entendres.

G. K. Chesterton: Lois alludes to a Chesterton quip on the pocket-knife being a secret sword (176). This quote comes from "What I Found in My Pocket," collected in *Tremendous Trifles* (1909).

Onomastics: Boyne (178) is a surname meaning "white cow" or the name of the Irish goddess of the River Boyne. The goddess was one of the Tuatha Dé Danann, the supernatural group that invaded Ireland.

4.07: (180) President Weer and Bill Batton in the presidential office, when the hair-covered man visits.

4.08: (180–91) Call from Lois wakes Weer. Visit to Blaine, where the tale of Tilly is concluded, and Weer looks through *The Lusty Lawyer.*

Timestamp: Visit to Blaine exposes his unreliable memories, including that Olivia gave Macafee the Chinese Egg, not at the man's 41st birthday party at Olivia's house (183), but at one of Judge Bold's Christmas parties before Prohibition (186). Blaine says he sold his house during the Great Depression (186), and that the town will revert to the Iroquois upon Blaine's death (187).

Dickens: *The Old Curiosity Shop* (1841) and *Nicholas Nickleby* (1839) are mentioned (190).

Thackeray: Mentioned (190).

4.09: (191–94) Meeting up with Lois outside library. Weer thinks on the killing of Olivia, of her infidelities, and of seeing her in the bath.

The Olivia Rant: From her death on the street (193) while freshly polluted with adultery, to her bathtub exposure of herself (194) like a wicked Bathsheba tempting David Copperfield.

Timestamp: Since the years are not given, from Olivia's marriage add two years before Den's parents returned from Europe (193).

4.10: (194) Weer breaks off to write how ill he is in the memory mansion.

4.11: (194–95) Aunt Bella and six-year-old Den at grandfather's house at Christmas.

Commentary: Denny writing his name and "words like 'cat' and 'rat'" (194) echoes back (or forward) to the "CAT" (90) of Doherty's story about St. Brandon's boat (88–91).

4.12: (195–98) Bella's published ghost story. Details of the hotel.

4.13: (198) Aside about definition of "bombardon."

4.14: (198–200) Ghost story continued. The strange events.

Commentary: The ghost-chaser story resolves cleanly as a time-travel event. When Bella exited her room and saw unusual lights and sounds outside, it was not anything so dramatic as a future nuclear holocaust, it was just a future street at night, typical in its time but busy beyond her imagining. At the same time, a guest from that future "all electric" time called the front desk because there were phantom candles around the bed, candles Bella had lit in her "limited electric" time frame.

Or maybe it was all just the work of pranksters.

4.15: (200) Weer intrudes.

4.16: (200) Weer has left his office room, now writes at table in Mab Crawford's kitchen.

4.17: (200–204) Gold's bookstore. Memoir by a missionary named Murchison. Buying the Kate Boyne diary. A week later, Lois invites Weer for dinner.

Little Orphant Annie: The poem "Little Orphant Annie" (1885) by James Whitcomb Riley is famous for being about a hired girl who tells goblin stories to children. It is called out by Lou Gold, who rightly says that Katie is just like Annie (203).

4.18: (204–206) Dinner at Lois's apartment.

4.19: (206–207) Margaret Lorn talking about the Bell Witch under her doorstep.

4.20: (207) Bill Batton talks with President Weer after Mrs. Porter visits about planting trees on graves, and after the visit by the hairy man.

Commentary: To summarize this day of three visitors, there is Bill Batton with his clockwork elephant, the hairy man, and Mrs. Eleanor Porter née Bold. Clearly the woman represents the future of the grave, and Bill Batton represents the present of the pocket circus.

4.21: (207–9) Lois calls, waking Weer.

4.22: (209–10) Quantrill and Kate Doherty née Boyne.

4.23: (210–11) Hunting for golden treasure.

4.24: (211–17) Weer goes to Gold's shop. He reveals the error in the diary.

Morryster: *Marvells of Science* is looked into, and Weer summarizes visions of heaven and hell (211). This book was invented by Ambrose Bierce for "The Man and the Snake" (1891), where the story quotes one line of text about snakes hypnotizing prey with their vision. The title was later used by Lovecraft in "The Festival" (1925).

D'Erlette: *Cultes des Goules* is examined, and Lou Gold says it is bound in human skin (213). This invented book appears in Lovecraft's "The Shadow Out of Time" (1935).

Shakespeare: Weer alludes to the famed "to be or not to be" meditation (215) in *Hamlet* (1600).

Onomastics: This is the time to note that Lorn (216) is an English surname meaning "forsaken."

Commentary: Gold has been forging books. This action matches the TAT Card ("[A] figure writes at a table, another peers over his shoulder") that set off the tale (166).

4.25: (217–19) Sherry Gold visits Weer at his apartment.

Onomastics: "Sherry" is from an Irish surname Ó Searraigh ("foal"), but it has been associated with French "cherie" (darling) as well as the fortified wine Sherry. This character's real name is Shirley (169), which is English for "bright wood," "bright meadow," or "from the white wood."

This is the time to mention that Arbuthnot (218) is a Scottish and Northern Irish surname meaning "healing river." So it appears that librarian Lois, with an Irish river in her name, was lured by the purported diary of a Boyne, named after an Irish river goddess.

4.26: (219–34) Weer takes Sherry to her house, meets with Gold. Talk about Venus of Melos as a forgery. The necromantic tale of the lich.

Venus of Melos: This conspiracy theory has a strong echo back to Cleopatra the Seal Girl, showing how she is a living version of the statue that "became a secret erotic stimulant for a whole generation of little boys—all over the world. Many men retain a lifelong interest in the things that stirred them as children" (226). This focus on the armless woman inverts the whole "men into statues" thread with a Pygmelion theme, where love for a statue is rewarded by the statue coming to life.

H. P. Lovecraft: When Gold says of one book, "A man over in Rhode Island made up the name" (231), he alludes to Lovecraft and the short story "The Hound" (1922), where the terrible tome *The Necronomicon* first appeared.

Necronomicon: The necromantic tale of the lich is from Gold's *Necronomicon,* but it seems like a story in the style of Clark Ashton Smith or Ambrose Bierce.

5. The President

5.01: Dr. Van Ness concludes the appointment, asks Weer to come back in the afternoon (235–36).

Back at the office, President Weer reads the letter from Charles Turner the Dog Man (236–42). The letter starts with Candy (238), then goes to her stepsister/half-sister Doris (238–42). Weer pushes the button for Miss Birkhead, but Miss Hadow comes in, as Miss Birkhead is ill (242). Weer and Miss Hadow examine the two photos, presumably of Candy (238) and Tom Lavine the Canadian Giant.

The other letter is from Professor Peacock to Julius Smart.

Weer decides to find the Persian room, but the hallway is the factory hallway. He meets Dan French and journalist Fred Thurlough who is at the plant for a tour (244). They decide to go in reverse order, starting at the cold house, where they tell the reporter about its haunting due to the Cold House Prank of 1938 (247–48).

Dan French tells Weer that Miss Birkhead says Weer drags one leg when tired (250), putting a timestamp on the stroke.

The spray towers are explained (258).

Returning to the office, Weer and Dan French learn that Miss Birkhead has died (261).

At Weer's request, Dan French tells the story about the last of the sidhe (261–63).

Weer wakes up at his desk, alone. Olivia's voice on the intercom says, "Den, darling, are you awake in there?"

Literary Lists: Charlie's letter gives Dickens's *David Copperfield* (1849); Jane Austen, Proust, Stendahl, and the great Russians (237).

Onomastics: "Turner" is usually an occupational name related to woodworking, but here, ironically, he was "turned" into a fake freak by his mother, Janet Turner. "Fred Thurlough" seems like a code for "thread furlough," which has mazy connotations.

Twain: *Life on the Mississippi* (1883) in the case of multiple copies for Charlie (237); the reporter mentions *Tom Sawyer* (1876) in reference to the Cold House Prank (247).

Onomastics: Birkhead (242) is an Old English name meaning "birch headland," but it is literally "birch head." "Taylor," Miss Birkhead's married name, is an Old English name for a maker or layer of tiles. "Hadow," Miss Birkhead's substitute, has a Scottish surname meaning "half a land measure," something like "halfacre."

Carney Girl Doris: Charlie's story is simple, but its intended message is ambiguous.

The simple part is a retelling of Cinderella with a downbeat ending. This story is a followup to the dinner conversation between Charlie and

Weer on the night of the three visitors (Batton, Charlie, and Eleanor).

The intended message should take into account this context, but even then some guesswork is required. For example, it seems probable that Charlie is a grifter, trying out several different leads to see what he can get. One unusual priority would be for him to discover if President Weer has the ability and the will to sell the same freak-making medicine that Mr. Tilly once did. But beyond that there is the everyday offer of underage women. By this light, it seems plain that Charlie is fishing for a "sugar daddy" for a sixteen-year-old girl who may not even exist yet. When Weer proved unreceptive to this, Charlie "killed" Doris and offered up her legal aged sister Candy (see sepia photo included). Even then, Weer smells a rat; he thinks the photos are of dead people, and presumably this means that Charlie is making up stories in some sort of con game.

Cold House Prank: Dan French is clear that he is using a ghost story as a bait for the reporter who is looking for human interest stories in the current labor conflict. He is trying to influence the reporter with the juicy tale of a greater sin in the distant past. While it is not a con game like Charles Turner's letter, it is still in a similar category of tempting the target with something easy and lurid.

Plant Engineering: This section of the novel, set at the factory, seems like a documentary on industrial processes, or plant engineering. No doubt this relates to the magazine *Plant Engineering* where Gene Wolfe worked as an editor from 1972 to 1986. Here Wolfe taps into the duality of being a plant engineer by day and author by night.

The Last of the Sidhe: Dan French's story is based upon the Irish legend of "The Children of Lir," but Lir had four children and they were turned into swans. Then there is Deirdre, the only named child in French's tale, who is named after the tragic heroine of a different Irish legend, her story being part of the Ulster Cycle.

Commentary: That Weer hears Olivia's voice over the desk intercom strongly suggests a massive change, a breakdown of reality boundaries. Earlier there is the confusion about the afternoon doctor's appointment, which was scheduled for the 45-year-old Weer, yet President Weer in his sixties still intends to go to it.

APPENDICES FOR PEACE

Appendix ADW1: Critics Speak

1986

Gordon, Joan. The *Peace* section of *Gene Wolfe: Starmont Reader's Guide 29,* 1986.

- Overview of novel.
- Situation of narrator: an old man casting back from a medical crisis, or a middle-aged man having a psychological crisis (31), or a boy having a poisoning crisis, passed out by his chemistry set (40).
- Similarity to *Slaughterhouse-Five* (33).
- Sense that the memoir ends unresolved (33).
- Was Weer truly responsible for Bobby's death? (34)
- Link between Olivia suitors and fairy tale (37).
- Novel contains at least thirteen embedded stories (38).

1996

Schuyler, William M. (Jr.). "Review of *Peace.*" *The New York Review of Science Fiction No. 89,* JAN 1996.

- Statement Weer born 1904 (19).
- Fairy tale and Olivia (20).

- Ben Yahya and Weer (20).
- Claim Weer haunted by cold house ghost (20).
- Interaction of TAT cards and stories (20).
- China pillow story.
- Smart's tale of Tilly.

Schuyler, William M. (Jr.). "Timeline for *Peace*." *The New York Review of Science Fiction No. 91,* MAR 1996.

- Weer born 1904.
- Includes birth years for Macafee, Olivia, Adelina, and Smart.

Broderick, Damien. "Thoughts on Gene Wolfe's *Peace*." *The New York Review of Science Fiction No. 91,* MAR 1996.

- Puts death of cold house prank on Weer (16).
- Linking of fairy tale to Olivia (16–7).
- Armless woman anticipating Thalidomide babies (17).
- Wolfe personally agreed that Peacock killed Olivia (17).
- Wolfe personally told him the juice is Tang (17).
- Wonder at the ghostly things Bella saw in her ghost-chaser assignment.

2006

Borski, Robert. "The Devil His Due," *The Long and the Short of It,* iUniverse, 2006.

- *Peace* and Goethe's *Faust* (17).
- Weer as the Devil (17).
- Margaret Lorn named after Faust's Margarete (20).
- Apple thread (21).
- Three suitors (23). Peacock kills Olivia (23; 25).
- Van Ness waiting room (27).
- Alchemical process in five stages.
- Ted Singer, or his father, as victim of the cold house prank (29).
- Smart as Tilly (24).

Borski, Robert. "The Coldhouse Prank," *The Long and the Short of It,* iUniverse, 2006.

- Ted Singer's father as victim in the cold house prank (31).
- Possible link Ted and Sherry (31).
- The Ted/Melissa bit (32).
- Weer's obsessive detailing of Ted's sporting and sexual activities like that of a surrogate father (33), casting Weer as a stalker.

Appendix ADW2: A Touchstone from Ambrose Bierce

"An Inhabitant of Carcosa" (1886)

Ambrose Bierce

For there be divers sorts of death—some wherein the body remaineth; and in some it vanisheth quite away with the spirit. This commonly occurreth only in solitude (such is God's will) and, none seeing the end, we say the man is lost, or gone on a long journey—which indeed he hath; but sometimes it hath happened in sight of many, as abundant testimony showeth. In one kind of death the spirit also dieth, and this it hath been known to do while yet the body was in vigor for many years. Sometimes, as is veritably attested, it dieth with the body, but after a season is raised up again in that place where the body did decay.

Pondering these words of Hali (whom God rest) and questioning their full meaning, as one who, having an intimation, yet doubts if there be not something behind, other than that which he has discerned, I noted not whither I had strayed until a sudden chill wind striking my face revived in me a sense of my surroundings. I observed with astonishment that everything seemed unfamiliar. On every side of me stretched a bleak and desolate expanse of plain, covered with a tall overgrowth of sere grass, which rustled and whistled in the autumn wind with heaven knows what mysterious and disquieting suggestion. Protruded at long intervals above it, stood strangely shaped and somber-colored rocks, which seemed to have an understanding with one another and to exchange looks of uncomfortable significance, as if they had reared their heads to watch the issue of some foreseen event. A few blasted trees here and there appeared as leaders in this malevolent conspiracy of silent expectation.

The day, I thought, must be far advanced, though the sun was invisible; and although sensible that the air was raw and chill my consciousness of that fact was rather mental than physical—I had no feeling of discomfort. Over all the dismal landscape a canopy of low, lead-colored clouds hung like a visible curse. In all this there were a menace and a portent—a hint of evil, an intimation of doom. Bird, beast, or insect there was none. The wind sighed in the bare branches of the dead trees and the gray grass bent to whisper its dread secret to the earth; but no other sound nor motion broke the awful repose of that dismal place.

I observed in the herbage a number of weather-worn stones, evidently shaped with tools. They were broken, covered with moss and half sunken in the earth. Some lay prostrate, some leaned at various angles, none was vertical. They were obviously headstones of graves, though the graves themselves no longer existed as either mounds or depressions; the years had leveled all. Scattered here and there, more massive blocks showed where some pompous tomb or ambitious monument had once flung its feeble defiance at oblivion. So old seemed these relics, these vestiges of vanity and memorials of affection and piety, so battered and worn and stained—so neglected, deserted, forgotten the place, that I could not help thinking myself the discoverer of the burial-ground of a prehistoric race of men whose very name was long extinct.

Filled with these reflections, I was for some time heedless of the sequence of my own experiences, but soon I thought, "How came I hither?" A moment's reflection seemed to make this all clear and explain at the same time, though in a disquieting way, the singular character with which my fancy had invested all that I saw or heard. I was ill. I remembered now that I had been prostrated by a sudden fever, and that my family had told me that in my periods of delirium I had constantly cried out for liberty and air, and had been held in bed to prevent my escape out-of-doors. Now I had eluded the vigilance of my attendants and had wandered hither to—to where? I could not conjecture. Clearly I was at a considerable distance from the city where I dwelt—the ancient and famous city of Carcosa.

No signs of human life were anywhere visible nor audible; no rising smoke, no watch-dog's bark, no lowing of cattle, no shouts of children at play—nothing but that dismal burial-place, with its air of mystery and dread, due to my own disordered brain. Was I not becoming again delirious, there beyond human aid? Was it not indeed *all* an illusion of my madness? I called aloud the names of my wives and sons, reached out my hands in search of theirs, even as I walked among the crumbling stones and in the withered grass.

A noise behind me caused me to turn about. A wild animal—a lynx—was approaching. The thought came to me: If I break down here in the desert—if the fever return and I fail, this beast will be at my throat. I sprang toward it, shouting. It trotted tranquilly by within a hand's breadth of me and disappeared behind a rock.

A moment later a man's head appeared to rise out of the ground a short distance away. He was ascending the farther slope of a low hill whose crest was hardly to be distinguished from the general level. His whole figure soon came into view against the background of gray cloud. He was half naked, half clad in skins. His hair was unkempt, his beard long and ragged. In one hand he carried a bow and arrow; the other held a blazing torch with a long trail of black smoke. He walked slowly and with caution, as if he feared falling into some open grave concealed by the tall grass. This strange apparition surprised but did not alarm, and taking such a course as to intercept him I met him almost face to face, accosting him with the familiar salutation, "God keep you."

He gave no heed, nor did he arrest his pace.

"Good stranger," I continued, "I am ill and lost. Direct me, I beseech you, to Carcosa."

The man broke into a barbarous chant in an unknown tongue, passing on and away.

An owl on the branch of a decayed tree hooted dismally and was answered by another in the distance. Looking upward, I saw through a sudden rift in the clouds Aldebaran and the Hyades! In all this there was a hint of night—the lynx, the man with the torch, the owl. Yet I saw—I saw even the stars in absence of the darkness. I saw, but was apparently not seen nor heard. Under what awful spell did I exist?

I seated myself at the root of a great tree, seriously to consider what it were best to do. That I was mad I could no longer doubt, yet recognized a ground of doubt in the conviction. Of fever I had no trace. I had, withal, a sense of exhilaration and vigor altogether unknown to me—a feeling of mental and physical exaltation. My senses seemed all alert; I could feel the air as a ponderous substance; I could hear the silence.

A great root of the giant tree against whose trunk I leaned as I sat held inclosed in its grasp a slab of stone, a part of which protruded into a recess formed by another root. The stone was thus partly protected from the weather, though greatly decomposed. Its edges were worn round, its corners eaten away, its surface deeply furrowed and scaled. Glittering particles of mica were visible in the earth about it—vestiges of its decomposition. This stone had apparently marked the grave out of which the tree had sprung ages ago. The tree's exacting roots had robbed the grave and made the stone a prisoner.

A sudden wind pushed some dry leaves and twigs from the uppermost face of the stone; I saw the low-relief letters of an inscription and bent to read it. God in Heaven! *my* name in full!—the date of *my* birth!—the date of *my* death!

A level shaft of light illuminated the whole side of the tree as I sprang to my feet in terror. The sun was rising in the rosy east. I stood between the tree and his broad red disk—no shadow darkened the trunk!

A chorus of howling wolves saluted the dawn. I saw them sitting on their haunches, singly and in groups, on the summits of irregular mounds and tumuli filling a half of my desert prospect and extending to the horizon. And then I knew that these were ruins of the ancient and famous city of Carcosa.

•

Such are the facts imparted to the medium Bayrolles by the spirit Hoseib Alar Robardin.

Commentary: This story, famous for having inspired Robert W. Chambers's *The King in Yellow* (1895) only a few years later, is clearly an essential seed for Wolfe's novel *Peace.*

Context: "An Inhabitant of Carcosa" was not first published in a genre magazine, since such things did not yet exist. It appeared in a standard newspaper in California. Because of this fact, I infer that the first readers took "Carcosa" to be the name of a California city (it certainly sounds like the name of a Californian city); and since there was no city of that name, it must be a future city (or the time-changed name of a current city). Robert W. Chambers definitely got into the future paradox nature with "The Repairer of Reputations," set 25 years in the future and describing a future New York City that might or might not exist.

Elements: The bewildered ghost. The sense that he had been ill. The invasion of the grave by the great tree. The reading of his name in the gravestone clutched by the tree's roots. The revelation that the great city is now a wasteland populated by animals and barbarous savages.

Strange Religion: The sense of antiquity to the setting is undercut by refusal to use familiar antique names of gods and prophets. While the narrator calls out for his plural wives, he does not use the term "Allah"; he uses "God" and "God in Heaven." Along with the obvious Spiritualism in the story, there might be a hint of Mormonism here. The strangeness seems to show up in *Peace* during the "unborn races" rant, talking about "strange oaths" and "What is a wabe?" (17)

Onomastics: The author Hali, who is quoted at the beginning, appears to be a fabrication by Bierce. While "Hali" in Greek means "from the sea," in Hebrew it means "sickness; a beginning; a precious stone," which seems far more appropriate.

Bayrolles the medium has a unique name which might point to California again, perhaps the San Francisco Bay.

Hoseib Alar Robardin, the ghost. "Hoseib Alar" seems like "José Ibalar;" "Alar" is Old French for "traveler;" "Robardin" looks vaguely Arabic, similar to Saladin.

Appendix ADW3: Timeline for *Peace*

Year	Age	Event
1799		The Egg appears in China.
1803		Ohio statehood.
1820		Venus de Milo discovered.
1850		(circa) Hannah Mill born.
1863		Quantrill's Lawrence Massacre.
1872		Date on silver dollar found by Den at picnic (216).
1888		Alleged publishing date of Murchison memoir, missionary in Tartary (201).
1914	born	Alden Dennis Weer is born in May.
1918	4	Denny sees Dr. Black; mother reading *Liberty* magazine.
1919	5	THE BLACK YEAR
1920		Prohibition begins.
1920	6	Christmas at grandfather's house.
1923	9	THE YEAR OF THE EGG HUNT
1924	10	THE CHEMICAL WEDDING
1926	12	Den sees Olivia in bath; Ludwig's biography of Napoleon translated; Den's parents return from Europe.
1928	14	Lou Gold leaves Germany for Britain.
1930	16	Den (presumably) hunting with his father John Weer (17; 249).
1931	16	Picnic with Margaret Lorn as high school junior, before May.
1933		Prohibition ends.

Year	**Age**	**Event**
1934	20	Den buys car as college junior; Olivia killed.
1938	24	THE COLD HOUSE PRANK
1939	25	Den's Chinese Garden Dream (death of Peacock?).
1950?		FURTHER DECLINE
1959	45	THE GOLD HUNT
1963	49	THREE VISITORS
1964	50	Dan French gives President Weer the box on behalf of the company.
1974	60	THE STROKE AND AFTER

THE BLACK YEAR

1) The women forge the treaty.
2) Den pushes Bobby Black down the stairs.

THE YEAR OF THE EGG HUNT

1) Bobby Black dies when Den was "eight or nine" which translates to the year when Den was eight before his birthday in May and nine after.
2) Den's parents go to Europe, leaving him with Aunt Olivia.
3) Olivia's suitors and the Chinese Egg.
4) Den and Maggie find the Egg on a Sunday in July.
5) Macafee's birthday party on August 3 (p. 80), where Olivia gives him the Egg and meets Julius Smart.

CHEMICAL WEDDING

1) Daffodils feature on the flower girl, and these flowers bloom in late winter/early spring.

FURTHER DECLINE (age unknown: between 25 and 38)

1) Weer's father dies. Weer continues to live in the house with his mother.
2) Weer's mother dies, after which he sells the house and moves into a small apartment.

THE GOLD HUNT

1) Weer is an engineer with Aaron Gold; it has been 25 years since Olivia's death, and Uncle Julius hasn't spoken to him in all that time.
2) Ted Singer is also around the office, and presumably talks about his sexual conquests Melissa and Lisa back in high school.
3) After decades of service Weer finds again his love, Margaret reborn as Sherry.

THREE VISITORS

1) Weer is suddenly a rich man: Julius Smart dies and the factory passes to Weer.
2) The "blue plans" (38) for the memory mansion are unrolled in Weer's small apartment, showing the speed of change.
3) Bill Batton arrives at the presidential office to talk about advertising campaign; Charlie Turner, the dog man, arrives unexpectedly; and Eleanor Porter (née Bold) interrupts regarding proposed planting of the elm tree upon Den's grave.

THE STROKE AND AFTER

1) Weer has stroke at age 60, the day after Sherry Gold dies.
2) Afterward he still works at the factory. On the day with Dan French and the reporter, Miss Birkhead is sick, so Miss Haddow is substituting for her. After the plant tour, Weer learns that Miss Birkhead has died, and Miss Hadow angles for her job.
3) He dies and is buried at the memory mansion with an elm tree planted on his grave.
4) Centuries pass until a storm blows over the massive elm.

Appendix ADW4: The Olivia Smart Chimera

Olivia is a composite creature. A bookish bohemian, she starts off as Auntie Mame, the heroine of Patrick Dennis's novel *Auntie Mame: An Irreverent Escapade* (1955). Set in the Roaring Twenties, it begins when a wealthy widower dies and leaves his ten-year-old son to his sister Mame, a flapper. The boy, named Patrick Dennis, sees her courtship rituals with a number of men. The cigarette holder is one of her symbols, along with high culture and madcap adventures.

This persona is aided and abetted by the unfinished fairy tale of the Princess and Her Three Suitors. While the princess story seems authentic, like something in an Andrew Lang collection, it is slyly subversive. After identifying the princess with Olivia, it proceeds to imply that the princess is a man-killing monster, perhaps more "Melusine" than "Maid Maleen."

The antics of the archeology and the artistry of the Nankeen Nook give way to the climax of the Egg Hunt. But Olivia is outfoxed by Macafee, and her persona takes a turn when Julius Smart enters the scene.

Olivia had set up the story telling game in a nod to Persian Shahrazad, but Julius Smart wins her with his words alone, in telling the dog boy story. The prophecy of the wolfskin-wearing wizard regarding Elaia, that "fire would win her," seems to have come true for Olivia. She marries Smart, and her American Auntie Mame is transmuted into the Japanese Princess Kaguya, heroine of "The Tale of the Bamboo Cutter."

Kaguya is a princess with many suitors, but none of them are good enough, so she gives them impossible tasks. Then the Mikado, the Emperor of Japan, comes along, and he wins her automatically. But Kaguya is sad, and she reveals that she is from the Moon, and will soon have to go back. Eventually the Moon people come and take her away. Responding to this, the Mikado orders that his letters to Kaguya be burned on the peak of Mount Fuji, so that the smoke might go through the air to reach her on the Moon.

Olivia follows this pattern. She awards herself to Smart, who is identified in the text with the emperor Napoleon (see Appendix ADW6). She grows matronly in dimensions, but not in pregnancy, and she has an adulterous affair with James Macafee in the sight of the Chinese Egg until she is murdered in a hit-and-run by Professor Peacock. Peacock dies, Smart dies, and Macafee presumably dies, but Blaine, the suitor of the air, becomes obsessed with honoring Olivia through a rare book collection at the place that was formerly her house.

The Olivia story starts out as comedic *Auntie Mame* but then switches over into the tragic form of "The Tale of the Bamboo Cutter."

Appendix ADW5: The Alden Dennis Weer Chimera

Like Olivia, Weer is a composite character, but his disguise is deeper.

At nine, Den plays the role of ward to his eccentric aunt just like ten-year-old Patrick Dennis to his Auntie Mame. Abandoned by his parents, he clearly makes his aunt and uncle into his new role models.

During the Egg Hunt, nine-year-old Maggie seems like a mini-Olivia, adventuring beside him. Den sees Maggie next at Olivia's wedding. At sixteen Den and Margaret become high school sweethearts. Den uses the same tale that Julius used to win Olivia, but it backfires horribly, and decades later he still wonders why.

Thirty years later he is working for Big Orange. At forty-five his life is in a rut; he has no love life. He is like a hardboiled detective: single, bitter, and getting too old. Then a case comes up.

Stop right there for a moment. The encrypted fact that he has been working for Big Orange for thirty years (education included) sends up a signal. Like a time-release drug, the story backs into connecting Weer to another fairytale fragment, the tale of ben Yahya and the marid. On the car drive to the Lorn farm, Den saw a pillar cloud in the sky, and he associated it with the genie coming out of the bottle found by the fisherman. There, on the verge of meeting Maggie, he repeats the tale of the hard worker who falls in love at first sight, then is promised his true love after he works for thirty years.

By this reading, the Gold Hunt is a mashup of Arabian Nights and hardboiled detective. The city has become haunted to Weer. Lois works at the library that was Olivia's house, and she seems like Olivia/Margaret. The Gold Hunt echoes the Egg Hunt, but this time the woman pulls a gun. Weer visits Lou Gold to tell him the error of his forgery, but the next thing that happens changes the story completely.

When Sherry Gold successfully seduces Weer, she retroactively changes his story to Nabokov's *Lolita* (1955), where Weer has been cast in the role of Humbert Humbert. With this new reading, Weer's imprint of nine-year-old Maggie is exactly like Humbert's imprint of nine-year-old Annabel Leigh, who tragically died of disease. The re-creation of the Egg Hunt as the Gold Hunt is like Humbert's attempt to recapture that "kingdom by the sea" with Lolita. And Sherry has links to Margaret at sixteen, as well as Shahrazad herself.

Through this transformational process, the sidekick nephew of *Auntie Mame* grows up through an Arabian Nights youth and a bitter noir middle age to emerge as the villain of *Lolita.*

Appendix ADW6: The Julius Smart Chimera

Julius Smart is more obscure than Olivia or A. D. Weer.

His name "Julius" echoes Julius Caesar, the man who nearly became emperor. Early in the text he is identified with another emperor: "While I was still living with my aunt Olivia, her husband bought her a Dresden figure of Napoleon for her mantle" (2). This seems to say that Smart is a "china emperor," or master of Olivia's personal "China."

But there is more to it than that.

If Julius is Napoleon, then Olivia is Josephine. This simple comparison shows unusual similarities between the two couples: Josephine was six years older than Napoleon, and Olivia seems exactly the same; Josephine had scandalous affairs after marriage, and Olivia also; Josephine did not produce a child with Napoleon, and Olivia seems to be in the same situation.

The most interesting bit is that Napoleon's successor, the French Emperor Napoleon III, was his nephew. Weer becomes Smart's nephew when Oliva marries Smart.

What does this say about Smart's mentor Tilly?

Tilly is a weird monster-maker, a "comprachicos" of the chemical kind, combining the powers of Medusa, Circe, and werewolf, all in one mild-mannered alchemist. If Julius is Napoleon, is Tilly somehow the French Revolution itself? Reducing humans to monsters, and then murdered by its own excesses?

Appendix ADW7: Fun and Crimes across the Times

There is a pattern to the fall of Bobby Black when Denny was five, and the cold house prank when Weer was 24. For one thing, both were witnessed by others.

There were children at Denny's party aside from Den and Bobby, girls and boys (4). While we do not know their names, we can guess some by the women who were there. The women are Mrs. Weer, Mrs. Black, Eleanor Bold, Hannah Mill, Olivia, Mrs. Singer, and Mrs. Green. That is seven women, but since Eleanor Bold, Hannah Mill, and Olivia have no children at this stage, Mrs. Singer and Mrs. Green probably bought multiple children each.

The cold house prank was cooked up by a group, probably fueled by alcohol. It looks like a class warfare action, of management versus workers. Weer was left behind to let the worker out; Weer was the one who took the blame, who paid the price.

There may be clues for co-conspirators among the photos on the wall in the memory mansion. There is Fred Neely (236), but he was a technician after Ron Gold. More probable is Bert Wise, an engineer (236).

But I look for those who have obviously advanced, leading me to speculate that the executive vice presidents Dale Everitton and Charlie Scudder (145) were the co-conspirators. Their careers advanced while Weer's was held back. This presumed guilt on their parts may explain why Charlie would dare to go into the blue-collar bar where President Weer worried that Charlie's tires might get slashed (162).

Appendix ADW8: Notes on Alchemy

The novel *Peace* has a rising tide of alchemical details even before the title of the central section "The Alchemist." The fairy tale of the princess and her three suitors lists earth, water, air, and fire, all potent elements of alchemy; and the curious Chinese Egg becomes a sort of philosopher's stone. Then "The Alchemist" tells of haunted Mr. Tilly, who achieves magical ends through pharmaceutical methods, a surprising sort of everyday alchemy, but the section also tells of Olivia's marriage to Julius Smart, which looks like a "chemical wedding" that produces the orange-drink empire practically overnight. The factory itself, with its eighteen-foot tall glowing orange, turns potatoes into gold.

So going back to Oliva and her suitors, there seems to be an alchemical level, almost a chemical recipe.

Alchemy is about creating a philosopher's stone. Alchemy has the four elements (earth, water, air, and fire) but it also has four stages or processes that are color-coded (blackness, whiteness, yellowness, and redness).

Olivia goes with her earth suitor and there is a blackness to her tablecloth. Olivia goes with her water suitor and there is whiteness with the porcelain she paints. This activity leads to clues about the Chinese Egg, which prompts Olivia to get money from her air suitor, Blaine (whose name means "yellow"). In complicated process or contest with water, Olivia wins the white stone but then surrenders it back to the water suitor. But at just that moment the fire suitor enters the stage. Olivia gives herself to him in marriage and the redness of Big Orange comes forth.

Big Orange is a philosopher's stone. It produces powdery red sulfur. It glows at night like an artificial sun.

Yet Olivia continues to search. She returns to her water suitor again and again, until she is killed by her earth suitor. Her earth suitor dies, probably poisoned by her husband, the fire suitor.

Appendix ADW9: The Mr. Tilly Chimera

The tale of haunted Mr. Tilly feels like a mashup of three threads: the novel *The Island of Doctor Moreau* (1896) by H. G. Wells; the pre-code motion picture *Freaks* (1932) by Tod Browning; and something hardboiled about gangsters kidnapping a doctor in the 1920s.

Doctor Moreau's transformational power is the basic thing.

Browning's *Freaks* has sideshow performers, of course, but it also involves a long-term poisoning: Cleopatra, a trapeze artist, learns that Hans the dwarf has a large inheritance, so she conspires with circus strongman Hercules. Her plan is to marry Hans, then kill him. She follows through on this by seducing him, and marrying him, at which point she begins poisoning him. Hans figures it out but becomes ill from the poison. He recovers and ultimately has his "freak-making" revenge upon Cleopatra and Hercules.

The gangster angle is more nebulous. The armless woman Jan, her driver, the Pierce-Arrow car, and her muscleman Clarence all give a sense of being gangsters. When they grab Smart and drive out to their place it is the familiar tableau of gangsters taking a doctor for healing a wounded comrade. The perceived ranking of the armless woman within the gang hierarchy develops slowly: when she first appears to pick up the drugs, it seems she is being looked after for being helpless; when she next appears on the occasion of kidnapping Smart, she clearly has a lot of power, so maybe she is the boss's moll; yet it turns out that the circus owner is the driver, and this seems to prove that Jan herself is the boss.

The tale of Tilly is highly fragmented. Most of it, broken up by interruptions, is given in "The Alchemist," but the ending is not given until Blaine talks to Weer in "Gold." Even so, the beginning context is obscure until a chance remark by Lou Gold about Venus of Melos hints at a fascinating key: that the armless statue "became a secret erotic stimulant for a whole generation of little boys . . . Many men retain a lifelong interest in the things that stirred them as children" (226).

I propose that Tilly was such a man, that the seal girl Jan was his personal sex goddess Venus. (Note the reversal: Weer's nightmares about anonymous men turning into statues versus a world-famous Venus statue coming to life.) To win her approval, Tilly created the freak-making drugs. I speculate that Tilly tested these chemicals first on his dog ("In back was a doghouse, but no sign of a dog" (132)), then on his son Rodney, and finally on his wife, killing each in turn.

This interpretation makes a hash out of Janet's self-given story, wherein she implies this is the first time she used Tilly's drugs; that she had heard about Tilly when she was with another organization where the dwarf talked about a treatment from Tilly three years earlier (153). But if she is a grifter, then such lies would be relatively easy for her.

She seems twenty (147), and if Charlie really is her son, she birthed him at age sixteen.

In case this theory seems to be a stretch, consider again Charlie's letter to President Weer, which is a sugar daddy lure that failed where Jan succeeded.

I propose the following solution to the remaining mystery of the ghost. The ghost is real, despite Blaine's assertion that the wife was a living poisoner until she drowned by accident. As a ghost, she moves unseen, but how does she achieve her poisoning at a restaurant or at home? Mr. Tilly supposes the ghost to have "a bottle of it somewhere" (158), but I insist she is dripping the stuff: this is the reside Smart notices on his bedsheet (137-38).

Appendix ADW10: *Peace* and the TAT Cards

The Thematic Apperception Test, developed in the 1930s, uses a series of cards with images to encourage patients to spontaneously generate stories. Initially there were 31 cards (one of them blank), each with a number and many having a code (B for "boy," F for "female," G for "girl," and M for "male").

In *Peace* there are two TAT cards used by Dr. Van Ness in his meeting with Weer. On the first, introduced at the beginning of "The Alchemist" section, a woman is handing something to another person (116). On the second card, shown at the start of the "Gold" section, a figure writes at a table while another person peers over his shoulder (166). Both cases show a story endpoint (Olivia handing the Chinese Egg to Macafee; Weer discovering Gold at his forgery), an orientation that seems opposite the notion of the card starting a story.

Weer describes the two TAT cards at the prompting of Dr. Van Ness, but there is a hint that Weer had previously responded to an earlier card that was not described. The last words of the first section are: "Turn over the first card. Tell me who the people are and what they are doing" (40). There is no talk of an image, but the "Olivia" section begins.

Research on the TAT cards reveals two surprises: the two cards described by Weer do not seem to be from the original set of TAT cards; but at least six of the real TAT cards show strong connections to the novel.

Relating to "1. Alden Dennis Weer":

Picture 8BM "A young boy in the foreground is staring directly out of the picture. In the background is a hazy image of two men performing surgery on a patient who is lying down."

This drawing seems to capture the fate of Bobby Black. The image of the boy wearing formal clothes in the foreground is the portrait of four-year-old Uncle Joe, or perhaps five-year-old Denny; the surgery is being performed on Bobby Black after the accident.

Relating to "2. Olivia":

Picture 17BM "A naked man is climbing up (or down) a rope."

This sketch recalls Professor Peacock climbing up and down the rope to the cave. The cave episode certainly formed the end of Peacock's courtship with Olivia. Perhaps this is the real TAT card that Weer saw after Dr. Van Ness told him to "Turn over the first card."

Relating to "3. The Alchemist":

Picture 12M "A man with his hand raised is standing above a boy who is lying on a bed with his eyes closed."

This image seems just like that point in the tale of Tilly where Julius Smart was sleeping and the wet ghost loomed over him.

Relating to "4. Gold":

Picture 13MF "A young man is standing in the foreground with his head in his arms. In the background is a woman lying in a bed."

This illustration matches the epilogue to the tale of Tilly, where Blaine mentions how Smart found the dead Mrs. Tilly in the locked bedroom.

Picture 2 "Country scene with a woman holding a book in the foreground. In the background, a man is working a field while a woman watches."

This image of female literacy at the hardworking farm encapsulates the Kate Boyne diary.

Relating to "5. The President":

Picture 12BG "A country setting depicts a tree, with a rowboat pulled up next to it. No human figures are present."

This illustration hauntingly suggests not only the emblematic elm tree but also the unearthed coffin (the rowboat).

•

Here is a description of the full set of TAT Cards (31 total).

1 Boy with violin.

2 Woman with book.

3BM Boy huddled at couch.

3GF Woman in anguish at door.

4 Woman grabbing shoulders of man turning away.

5 Woman looking into room from a doorway.

6BM An elderly woman is standing by a window, a younger man behind her.

6GF A young woman sitting on a sofa being addressed by an older man.

7BM An older man looking at a younger man who is peering into space.

7GF A girl is sitting on a sofa with a doll, a woman is reading to her.

8BM A young boy in the foreground is staring directly out of the picture.

8GF A woman is sitting in a chair staring into space.

9BM Four men in a field are lying against one another.

9GF A woman is standing behind a tree, watching another woman running by.

10 One person holding his or her head against another person's shoulder.

11 On a road in a chasm, several figures on a path.

12BG A country setting.

12F A woman in the foreground, an older woman in the background.

12M A man with his hand raised above a boy on a bed.

13B A boy is sitting in the doorway of a log cabin.

13G A girl is climbing a flight of stairs.

13MF A young man is standing with his head in his hands.

14 A person is silhouetted against a window.

15 A man is standing among tombstones with his hands clasped together.

16 Blank card.

17BM A naked man is climbing up (or down) a rope.

17GF A female is standing on a bridge over water.

18BM A man is being grabbed from behind. Three hands are visible.

18GF A woman is choking another woman by a flight of stairs.

19 A surreal depiction of clouds and a home covered with snow.

20 A nighttime picture of a man leaning against a lamppost.

Appendix ADW11: Notes on "The Changeling"

"The Changeling" is a short story first published in Damon Knight's *Orbit 3* (1968), collected in *Gene Wolfe's Book of Days* and omnibus *Castle of Days* (the hardcover edition cited hereafter). It offers the first glimpse of Cassionsville, here called "Cassonsville." It is the story of Crazy Pete, a character who is mentioned only in passing by Weer: "West of the town, in broader, quieter water, there is a long, stony island which used, at about the time I imagined myself visiting Dr. Van Ness, to harbor a hermit called Crazy Pete" (*Peace,* 48).

Synopsis: The narrator Pete intends to leave this manuscript in the dry cave.

He writes that he was in Korea when the Korean War started. He was captured but refused repatriation during the prisoner exchange. After some years in China, he changed his mind and was repatriated. He was one of the few to face trial, and then he served time at Ft. Leavenworth. Upon release he went to visit Cassonsville, the town of his childhood.

The place has not changed, but the weird thing is that little Peter Palmieri has not changed at all: he is still eight or nine years old. In the Palmieri house he was first the older brother, then twin brother to Maria, then the middle child (the stage when he wrestled with narrator Pete that time), then presumably twin to Paul, and now the little brother.

Narrator Pete tries to figure out this mystery, but only finds more mysteries. The local paper has no word about his own Korean shame, nor is there mention of his birth; in his fourth-grade class picture, Peter Palmieri is there, but narrator Pete is not.

Pete retreats to the island and stays there. He suggests that the eternal boy Peter is, in fact, Peter Pan.

Commentary: It is a spooky story of a person seeking comfort in his old haunts, yet he finds only cosmic alienation instead.

Reading the story, there are many different models for "the changeling," yet each remains elusive, in part because the definition of a changeling as a fairy child swapped for a human child is not clearly met. Instead there is a dopplegänger, an unperson, missing time, community amnesia, and a reality-bending perpetual child.

This version of Peter Pan is far removed from the usual. The idea of Pete and Peter having fought and separated finds a sort of analogy to the episode when Peter Pan lost his shadow.

Pete's experience in Korea and China seem close to a nightmarish excursion in fairy lands, a dark version of Thomas Rhymer or Rip Van Winkle.

Year	Event
1944	Pete is in fourth grade (168), presumed nine or ten years old. He and his father move away the month before fifth grade starts.
1945	The old newspaper burned, losing older records.
1950	Pete with US Army in Korea, "helping a captain teach demolition" (160). This implies he is at least seventeen, which seems one or two years off.
1953	The prisoner exchange (170) which Pete refused.
1959	Pete searches for news in August and September of 1959 (169), presumably relating to his return to the USA and his trial.
196_	Pete returns to Cassonsville.

A changeling is defined as "An ill-favored, deformed, huge-headed, or imbecilic child, believed to be the offspring of fairies . . . and supposed to have been substituted by them for a normal or beautiful one stolen away in infancy" (*Funk & Wagnalls Standard Dictionary of Folklore, Mythology, and Legend*).

Under "fairy," other details emerge: "Fairies often abduct mortals. . . . Many believe that the fairies must pay a yearly tribute to the lords of hell by sending some of their number there each year. For this purpose they are thought to abduct mortals, especially children. Tam Lin, a mortal abducted by the fairies in the Scotch ballad, was to be so sacrificed but his sweetheart succeeded in rescuing him" (ibid, 364).

Also "A few stories tell of changelings growing up among mortals; usually they are deformed in some way, but always they are beautiful of face; often they are endowed with some extraordinary ability" (365).

•

A different solution would be if Cassonsville were fairy land, with our world as their hell.

THE DEVIL IN A FOREST

Edition cited: Follett (hb) 40667-1, 9-76, 224pp, $5.95 (David Palladini)

Epigraph: From "Good King Wenceslas" (1853), an English Christmas carol about a Bohemian king and his page enduring harsh winter conditions while going to give alms to a peasant.

Prologue: (9–12) A peddler stops at a farmhouse, sells some items, and finds out about the settlements along a fork in the road. He goes back to investigate and is abruptly murdered, his last thoughts being on his childhood in Prague.

One: (13–20) At the peddler's funeral is the abbé, along with Old Paul the Sexton, Gloin the Weaver, Mark the weaver's apprentice, and Cope the Smith. They speculate that Wat killed the peddler.

Fourteen-year-old Mark meets his barmaid girlfriend Josellen. She tells him that Mother Cloot, the witch, has entered the taproom with the abbé.

Two: (21–34) Mark goes to the taproom. The abbé has called a meeting to discuss the bad influence of Wat. Wat's character is defended by a nameless charcoal burner. Philip the Cobbler tells of seeing Wat at a fair. Cope tells of shoeing a horse for Wat.

The abbé proposes the formation of a village militia.

Local History: The abbé says that for three hundred years the area was ravaged by Vikings (24). The charcoal burner says his people have a statue of the Virgin that used to stand in Grindwalled (24).

Three: (35–49) Mark, scrounging for food at night, meets Josellen. Together they go hiking to find Mother Cloot. They find her at Miles Cross, an ancient barrow. She invites them to her house and rides Mark's shoulders. They pass through Grindwalled, the ruins of a village. Mother Cloot's home is a tree house. It turns out Wat is sleeping there.

Bible: Children who mocked a prophet were eaten by a bear (43). This is about Elisha and the two bears, an incident in the Old Testament:

> And he went up from thence unto Bethel: and as he was going up by the way, there came forth little children out of the city, and mocked him, and said unto him, Go up, thou bald head; go up, thou bald head.
>
> And he turned back, and looked on them, and cursed them in the name of the LORD. And there came forth two she bears out of the wood, and tare forty and two children of them. (2 Kings 2:23–24)

Baba Yaga: Mark sees Mother Cloot's tree house and remembers a story about a witch having a house raised up on four giant chicken legs (49). Baba Yaga is a famous witch in Slavic folklore, and her hut standing on chicken legs is her premier symbol.

Four: (50–58) In the morning Wat gets to know the youngsters. He sends Josellen with a message for the abbé and holds Mark as hostage. Then Wat leads Mark to find Gil the charcoal burner.

Five: (59–71) They find the camp of the charcoal burners. Mark sees the blackened statue he supposes must be of the Virgin Mary, but Wat says it might be Freyr or Freya.

Wat and Gil discuss things. Gil equips Mark with an axe and they travel downhill in a coracle boat. Near Mark's village they find a body hanging from a tree, and it is Paul the Sexton. Wat admits to killing the peddler but swears he did not kill Paul. Wat notes that Paul was killed, buried, then dug up and displayed.

Wat sends Mark to ask Paul's wife if there is ambush set against Wat.

Myth: Freyr and Freya, mentioned by Wat (61), are Vanir gods from Norse myth.

Six: (72–81) Mark goes to Paul's house. Mother Cloot is already there. Mark gets spooked and leaves. He overhears Mother Cloot reading runes and it sounds like she is framing him for Paul's murder. Alarmed, he goes to Paul's corpse, hauls it to the river, and tosses it in, along with the axe. He goes to the shrine to pray, then to the taproom, where Josellen urges him to join the meeting.

Rune Sticks: These are tiny bones, like twigs, but Mother Cloot says they are thigh bones of men (75), "Murdered by me and their mothers" (76). They are from abortions.

Seven: (82–95) The meeting at the tap room shifts with the arrival of Mark, proving he is alive and well. Wat asks for assistance before he leaves the area, and it amounts to help in the road robbery of a specific rich pilgrim. This talk is interrupted by the arrival of Old Sue and Mother Cloot, who discovered the corpse of Paul in the river, and Mother Cloot charges Mark with the murder.

The abbé, through questioning, establishes that Mark received the axe after Paul was killed the previous night, before the others had gathered at the taproom.

After a tense standoff is broken by the innkeeper refusing to take sides, Wat convinces them to keep Mark close, as part of the robbery group.

Eight: (96–101) Gil, Gloin, and Mark are joined by Wat. Wat gives his interpretation on the abbé's talk, that the holy man was trying to hang Mark. Then Wat admits there is no pilgrim to rob: the real target is neighbor Philip the Cobbler.

Nine: (102–106) Mark's sleep is interrupted by a vivid nightmare or a vision about an ancient warrior waking up and coming forth into the village.

Ten: (107–13) Wat and Mark burgle Philip the Cobbler's house. Just as they are leaving, soldiers are going door to door.

Eleven: (114–20) Wat, Gil, and Mark hike. After further adventure, Mark breaks away from them, getting stabbed in the side.

Twelve: (121–28) Mark wakes up in the forest being tended by Josellen, the abbé, Old Sue, Gloin, and Philip. They had abandoned their village to the soldiers. They spend four days in the forest. The abbé goes alone to the village to see if the soldiers are still there.

Notes: The abbé talks about the White Monks (125). Historically, the white monks (the Order of Cistercians) began in 1098. The white monks appear, anachronistically, in Arthuriana, and may, in fact, have had a hand in shaping Arthuriana.

Thirteen: (129–40) In their sleep the campers are captured by soldiers, only Josellen and Gloin escaping. They are marched to the village. Philip, Philip's wife, Mark, and Old Sue are jailed in the inn's wine cellar. Mark and Philip fight until they discover Old Sue has died. Then the soldier takes Philip up. Someone begins screaming under torture.

Fourteen: (141–50) Mark is brought upstairs for food and friendly questioning by the leader, whom he calls "the Boar."

Fifteen: (151–56) Mark is beaten after all, then put in a little garret room up on the third floor. The innkeeper meets with him, tells him Jocellen and Gloin are hiding in the inn.

Sixteen: (157–66) The forester Sieur Ganelon comes to the village. The innkeeper has been beaten into paralysis. Sieur Ganelon leaves. The soldiers take Philip and set fire to his house on their way out of the village. Mark is joined by the abbé, who sends him to fetch Cope.

Seventeen: (167–75) Mother Cloot comes to the village. The group meets in the taproom, and move the head-injured innkeeper there. Cope will guard him against the witch while the abbé and Mark search for Gloin and Jocellen.

Eighteen: (176–90) As the two search they discuss paralysis to the best of their understanding. They return to the taproom to find the witch making claims, and Cope confesses to having hit the innkeeper before. They see the innkeeper has died. The abbé has Mark go over all the details to find the hiding place, and Mark figures it out.

Nineteen: (191–95) Morning comes. Mark goes outside. Josellen comes out carrying a sheepskin coat she has been making for him. They share time together, sitting on the steps.

Twenty: (196–201) Mark and the abbé make two coffins as Cope digs two graves. The few villagers remaining have their church time, then bury their friends. Suddenly they are surrounded by Wat and many charcoal burners.

Wat's eyes are strange when he says to Mark, "I am dreaming, and you are awake in my dream." This echoes Mark's dream of the Barrow Man.

Twenty-One: (202–11) Mark escapes from the prisoner line. He is chased through the night. He finds the soldier camp and makes a deal with the Boar. When they arrive at the village, they interrupt a weird ceremony of pagan sacred marriage.

Twenty-Two: (212–21) Sometime later in the city (presumably Prague?), Mark answers questions on the case from a nobleman. It seems that Wat was under the influence of Mother Cloot's mind-bending herbs, and under her instruction he thought himself possessed by the spirit of the Barrow Man.

The abbé was blinded by Mother Cloot. The authorities plan to execute Gloin as a spy for the bandit Wat. Gil the Burner will be executed for the murder of Old Paul and Cope.

Mark reveals that Wat was also Sieur Ganelon. As such, he was living a double life, but then it became a triple life when he thought he was the Barrow Man.

The burners' statue, claimed to be of the Virgin Mary, was really a pagan idol for the Barrow Man.

The nobleman gives Mark a gold coin.

Commentary: The conspiracy was decades in the making. The charcoal burners are presumably descendants of the town Grindwalled, a Viking settlement worshiping the Barrow Man. (I speculate that Grindwalled was smashed by a Christian king, perhaps Charlemagne during his war against the Saxons.) The burners financed Wat through seminary in order that he could take over the religious station of the village. Then as a bandit he whittled down the pilgrims, putting strain on the village, weakening it. When Jocellen was old enough to be a bride to the Barrow Man, the final phase was put into play, with more of the villagers killed. Clearly the charcoal burners were ready to move in as replacement villagers, and they would secretly live under their priest-king Wat, worshiping the Barrow Man.

Epilogue: (222) A modern American couple read a rock-carved monument. We learn that the abbé had his sight restored by the waters and is remembered as a saint.

About the Author: (223–24) The link to the Christmas carol "Good King Wenceslas" gives another epilogue to the story, suggesting that the novel is the "true background" to the song of the king and his page walking through snow to aid a peasant. That is, things are a little re-arranged: the peasant walked through the snow to the city; the noble heard his story of hardship, blessed his coming marriage, and gave him a gold coin.

Commentary: In turn, this bookending of the song gives a fix on the place and time of the novel being Bohemia, some year between 921 and 935. The reign of Wenceslas ended with his martyrdom, for which he was celebrated in Bohemia and England. The song, written in 1835, presents an episode (a peasant living near a St. Agnes' fountain) that is not based upon the saint's hagiography. Searching for a real St. Agnes' fountain within Bohemia is beside the point: it is in the song; the novel is based upon the song.

The mention of Prague relating to the peddler in the Prologue gives some support to the Bohemia side. The presence of the barrow gives a complicated result: most of the Czech burial barrows are Slavic, but there are also some prehistoric ones, the most famous being the hilltop from which Napoleon commanded his forces during the Battle of Austerlitz (Zuran Hill near Slavkov u Brna).

But the idea of Vikings harassing Bohemia for three hundred years seems a stretch, whereas the Vikings were certainly a presence in the British

Isles. The novel gives us Vikings on the Elbe; establishing Grindwalled; and zipping down the river in leather-and-wicker coracles (vehicles associated with the British Isles). The vision of the Barrow Man with chainmail seems rather Viking (certainly not "prehistoric"), along with Mother Cloot's mention of were-foxes in artwork inside the mound.

(Among the various anachronisms there is the sandwich that the abbé sups upon.)

By using such well-known figures as Vikings, the text reveals a slow-moving war between Christianity and Paganism. Christianity has a local representative with a site (the fountain), a community (the villagers), a spiritual leader (the abbé), and a champion (Mark); Paganism (the Vanir) has a site (the barrow), a community (the burners), a spiritual leader (Mother Cloot), and a champion (Wat). Framed this way, it looks a bit like a Christian "David" versus a Pagan "Goliath."

This battle reflects something from the household of the historical Wenceslas. His mother, originally from a pagan tribe, was anti-Christian during her Bohemian regency; and his younger brother murdered him to gain the throne. When the abbé compares Wat to the Vikings it is ironically prophetic, since it seems in the end that Wat, Mother Cloot, and the burners are all trying to claw back the reign of terror that was the old way. In the novel, Mark has a happy ending; in history, Duke Wenceslas had martyrdom.

APPENDICES FOR THE DEVIL IN A FOREST

Appendix DF1: Onomastics

Cloot: Scottish for a cloven hoof.

Cope: Oddly, the occupational name for one who makes cloaks or capes.

Frey and Freya: Twin deities of the Vanir, a family of gods distinct from the Æsir (with Odin, Thor, et alia). That their names mean "lord" and "lady" is "a circumstance suggesting connection with the cult of the sacred marriage in ancient West Asia" (Cotterell, *A Dictionary of World Mythology*), a link that seems proven in this novel.

Ganelon: Knight who betrayed Charlemagne's army to the Saracens, leading to the battle of Roncevaux Pass. Said to come from Italian "inganno," meaning fraud or deception.

Gil: Germanic "shaft of an arrow" or "pledge, hostage."

Gloin: Old Norse "glowing" from the lists of dwarfs in *Poetic Edda.*

Jocellen: Hebrew Jocelin "supplanter" or Latin Jocelyn "happy."

Mark: Latin "consecrated to the god Mars"; also one of the authors of the gospels, Mark the Evangelist. Yet I suspect the character's name comes from a line in the song: "*Mark* my footsteps, good my page."

Paul: Latin "small," "humble," but also a famous saint.

Philip: Greek "friend of horses," yet also one of the twelve apostles.

Sue: From Late Latin "Suzanna," meaning lily, rose.

Wat: English "hurdle" or Teutonic "strong fighter."

Appendix DF2: Vikings and Voodoo

The scenario with the Barrow Man and Wat and Mother Cloot has interesting ties to both Viking culture and Voodoo culture.

The Viking presence shows traces in the text with talk of Viking savagery and mention of Freyr and Freya, but in Norse myth there is more. H. R. Ellis Davidson notes, "The Vanir are represented as having close connexions with life in the burial mound . . . We know Freyr himself was said to have been laid in a mound, and to have rested there while offerings were made to him" (*Gods and Myths of Northern Europe,* p. 154). Having established Freyr as a nature and death god, she goes into further curious detail, giving us

> the story of an early king in Norway, called [after death] Olaf . . . 'elf of Geirstad.' We are told in *Flateyjarbók* that in time of famine men sacrificed to him in his howe [burial mound] for plenty, even as they were said to have done to Freyr. When Olaf the Holy was born, he was named after this earlier Olaf, his ancestor, and was given his sword and ring, said to have been taken out of the burial mound to be presented to the child at his birth. Consequently men believed that the second Olaf was the first reborn, although the Christian king sternly contradicted such rumors (155).

Olaf the Holy (995–1030), a patron saint of Norway, was thought by many to be a reincarnation of Olaf Geirstad-Alf (810–860), who had been worshiped after death in the style of Freyr the Vanir god. This shows a tremendous amount of tension between the old pagan ways and the more recent Christianity. Olaf insisted that his soul was unique to him, and not a return of his ancestor. Scripture is solid on this.

Gene Wolfe has shifted this scenario slightly, from a case of reincarnation to a type of possession. That is, Wolfe is examining the consequences of two persons being present in the one body, a situation that looks similar to the Voodoo zombie.

Zombies in Voodoo culture are different from zombies in the movies, in that they are mindless slaves of their masters. One theory of how this might work in real life is sketched out by Zora Neale Hurston in the "Zombies" chapter of *Tell My Horse* (1938). Hurston reports a pharmaceutical theory shared with her by medical doctors in Haiti: a secret society possesses two powerful drugs, one producing a death-like state, the other an antidote to the first. The zombie-master selects a living target and gives that person the first drug, then after that person is entombed, the master breaks into the tomb and administers the antidote. The zombie is used as a labor slave and is kept in a daily drugged state.

Gene Wolfe applies this pharmaceutical explanation to the Olaf reincarnation situation and arrives at *The Devil in a Forest.* It appears that Mother Cloot targeted Wat, training him through words and drugs, to the point where he would be possessed by the Barrow Man, in reality or only in his own mind.

In the text, Wat gives a drug-weakened Mother Cloot some strong wine as an antidote (54), saying that the herbs in her doeskin bag (55) would kill her in her debilitated state. When Mark encounters her not much later, he is surprised to see "vigor in every movement . . . her pupils were almost invisible" (73). Near the end of the novel, when Wat surprises the villagers at the graveyard, Mark notes, "There was something unnatural in Wat's eyes that reminded Mark of the way Mother Cloot looked at times" (201), which ties back to something Gil had said about Wat much earlier: "He does get spells upon him, though, when he's freer with his arrows and his knife than maybe his friends like to see him" (25). The trail of clues establish that Wat has a history of using drugs and displays shifting personalities as a result.

The most eerie scene is when the prisoners are led from the graveyard toward their doom:

> In his ear Wat said, "Mark, are you awake?"
>
> Not understanding what was meant, Mark could only nod.
>
> "That's strange," Wat whispered. "I am dreaming, and you are awake in my dream." Mother Cloot touched his arm, and he said no more. (201)

Here Wat shows he is a drugged zombie, controlled by the witch in whole or in part. This sense is reiterated after the ceremony is broken up: while being led away, Wat "looked toward the bowed figure of Mother Cloot as if for instructions or advice, but she did not lift her head" (211).

BIBLIOGRAPHY

Operation ARES

Brunner, John. *The Squares of the City*. 1965.
Burgess, Anthony. *A Clockwork Orange*. 1962.
Chesterton, G. K. *The Man Who Was Thursday*. 1908.
Gordon, Joan. *Gene Wolfe*. 1986.
Lewis, C. S. Narnia series.
Nowlan, Philip Francis. *Armageddon 2419 A.D.* 1928.
———. *Buck Rogers* serial. 1939.
Orwell, George. *Nineteen Eighty-Four.* 1949.
Wells, H. G. *The War of the Worlds*. 1898.
———. Orson Welles' radio broadcast of the above. 1938.

The Fifth Head of Cerberus

Borski, Robert. *The Long and the Short of It.* 2006.
Cabell, James Branch. (Poictesme novels.)
Čapek, Karel. "From the Point of View of a Cat." 1935.
Carroll, Lewis. *Through the Looking-Glass*. 1871.
Castaneda, Carlos. *The Teachings of Don Juan*. 1968.
Clute, John. "Gene Wolfe" entry in *The Encyclopedia of Science Fiction*. 1993.
Coleridge, Samuel Taylor. "The Rime of the Ancient Mariner." 1798.
Condon, Richard. *The Manchurian Candidate*. 1959.
de Camp, L. Sprague. "Viagens Interplanetarias" fictions.
Dick, Philip K. *Do Androids Dream of Electric Sheep?* 1968.
Dickens, Charles. *David Copperfield*. 1850.
Dumas, Alexandre. *The Three Musketeers*. 1844.
Euripides. *Heracles*.

Funnidos, Richum. *The Comic Almanack for 1841.*
Gordon, Joan. *Gene Wolfe.* 1986.
Hemingway, Ernest. "Indian Camp." 1924.
Homer. *The Odyssey.*
Hopkins, Gerard Manley. "The Loss of the Eurydice." 1918.
Kafka, Franz. *The Trial.* 1925.
Kipling, Rudyard. "The Strange Ride of Morrowbie Jukes." 1885.
Koestler, Arthur. *Darkness at Noon.* 1941.
Kurosawa, Akira. *The Seven Samurai.* 1954.
Le Guin, Ursula K. "Ekumen" fictions.
Lewis, Meriwether and William Clark. *The Journals of Lewis and Clark.* 1814.
Lovecraft, H. P. "The Shadow Out of Time." 1936.
MacRitchie, David. *The Testimony of Tradition.* 1890.
Nilsson, Sven. *The Primitive Inhabitants of Scandinavia.* 1868.
Plautus. *Aulularia.*
Poe, Edgar Allan. "The Black Cat." 1843.
———. "The Raven." 1845.
———. "The Sphinx." 1846.
Proust, Marcel. *Remembrance of Things Past.* 1913–1927.
Robinson, Kim Stanley. "A Story," *New York Review of Science Fiction No. 301.* 2013.
St. John of the Cross. *Ascent of Mount Carmel.*
Sargent, Pamela. Afterword to *The Fifth Head of Cerberus.* 1976.
Shakespeare, William. *The Merchant of Venice.* 1605.
Siegel, Don. *Invasion of the Body Snatchers.* 1956.
"Snow White and the Seven Dwarfs."
Vance, Jack. *The Star King.* 1964.
Verne, Jules. *Twenty Thousand Leagues Under the Sea.* 1870.
Virgil. *The Aeneid.*
Wilhelm, Kate. *The Mile-Long Spaceship.* 1963.
Wolfe, Bernard. *The Great Prince Died.* 1959.
Woolf, Virginia. *Monday or Tuesday.* 1921.

Peace

Arabian Nights.
Barrie, J. M. *Peter Pan.* 1904.
Bierce, Ambrose. "An Inhabitant of Carcosa." 1886.
———. "The Man and the Snake." 1891.
Borski, Robert. "The Devil His Due," *The Long and the Short of It,* 2006.
———. "The Coldhouse Prank," *The Long and the Short of It,* 2006.
Broderick, Damien. "Thoughts on Gene Wolfe's *Peace.*" *The New York Review of Science Fiction No. 91,* MAR 1996.

Browning, Tod. *Freaks.* 1932.
Cabell, James Branch. *Jurgen.* 1919.
Carroll, Lewis. "Jabberwocky." 1871.
Chesterton, G. K. *Tremendous Trifles.* 1909.
D'Erlette. *Cultes des Goules.*
Dante. *Paradiso.*
Dennis, Patrick. *Auntie Mame.* 1955.
Dickens, Charles. *David Copperfield.* 1849.
———. *Nicholas Nickleby.* 1839.
———. *The Old Curiosity Shop.* 1814.
Dostoyevsky, Fyodor. *Crime and Punishment.* 1866.
Funk & Wagnalls Standard Dictionary of Folklore, Mythology, and Legend.
Gilbert and Sullivan. *The Mikado.* 1885.
Glinka, Mikhail. *A Life for the Czar.* 1836.
Gordon, Joan. *Gene Wolfe.* 1986.
Japanese fairy tale. "The Tale of the Bamboo Cutter."
Lang, Andrew. *The Green Fairy Book.* 1892.
Lovecraft, H. P. "The Festival." 1925.
———. "The Hound." 1922.
———. "The Shadow Out of Time." 1935.
Loudan, Jack. *O Rare Amanda!* 1954.
Ludwig, Emil. *Napoleon.* 1926 (translated).
Montesquieu. *Persian Letters.* 1721.
Morris, William. *The Well at the World's End.* 1896.
Morryster. *Marvells of Science.*
Nabokov, Vladimir. *Lolita.* 1955.
The Necronomicon.
Poussin, Nicolas. *Et in Arcadia ego.* 1637.
Riley, James Whitcomb. "Little Orphant Annie." 1885.
Ros, Amanda. *Irene Iddesleigh.* 1897.
———. *Delina Delaney.* 1898.
———. *Donald Dudley.* 1900.
———. *Poems of Puncture.* 1912.
———. *Fumes of Formation.* 1933.
Schuyler, William M. (Jr.). "Review of *Peace.*" *The New York Review of Science Fiction No. 89,* JAN 1996.
———. "Timeline for *Peace.*" *The New York Review of Science Fiction No. 91,* MAR 1996.
Shakespeare, William. *Hamlet.* 1600.
———. *A Midsummer Night's Dream.* 1596.
Sutherland, John. *Curiosities of Literature.* 2009.
Trollope, Anthony. *Barchester Towers.* 1857.
Twain, Mark. *Life on the Mississippi.* 1883.

———. *Tom Sawyer.* 1876.
Vonnegut, Kurt. *Slaughterhouse-Five.* 1969.
Wallace, Lew. *Ben-Hur: A Tale of the Christ.* 1880.
Wells, H. G. *The Island of Doctor Moreau.* 1896.
Wolfe, Gene. "The Changeling." 1968.

The Devil in a Forest

Cotterell, Arthur. *A Dictionary of World Mythology.* Oxford Paperback Reference. Oxford University Press, 1986.
Davidson, H. R. Ellis. *Gods and Myths of Northern Europe.* Paperback. Penguin Books, Harmondsworth, England, 1964.
Hurston, Zora Neale. *Tell My Horse.* 1938.
Neale, John Mason. "Good King Wenceslas." 1835.
Norse poems. *Poetic Edda.*

ABOUT THE AUTHOR

Michael Andre-Driussi has produced a number of books about science fiction and fantasy works. His titles on Gene Wolfe's fiction are *Lexicon Urthus* (1994), *The Wizard Knight Companion* (2009), *Gate of Horn, Book of Silk* (2012), *Gene Wolfe: 14 Articles on His Fiction* (2016), and *Gene Wolfe's The Book of the New Sun: A Chapter Guide* (2019). With Alice K. Turner he co-edited *Snake's-Hands: The Fiction of John Crowley* (2001). His two books about Jack Vance's oeuvre are *Handbook of Vance Space* (2014) and *Jack Vance: Seven Articles on His Work and Travels* (2016). Branching out, he also has touched on Soviet science fiction with the popular *Roadside Picnic Revisited* (2016), being about the Strugatsky novel made into the Russian motion picture *Stalker* (1979), as well as a survey of Japanese animation in *True SF Anime* (2014).

Made in the USA
Middletown, DE
14 August 2020